# A Playground in Beijing

The 2024 anthology of poetry and prose by members of the Federation of Writers (Scotland)

Published 2024
By New Voices Press
Imprint of the Federation of Writers (Scotland)

©2024
All rights reserved. No part of this book may be reproduced, stored in a retrieval system, or transmitted in any form or by any means (electronic, mechanical, photocopy, sound or digital recording) or translated into any language, without prior written permission from the Federation of Writers (Scotland), except by a reviewer who may quote brief passages in a review.

The rights of the contributors to be identified as the authors of their work in this book have been asserted by them in accordance with Section 77 of the Copyright, Designs and Patents Act 1988.

# Federation of Writers (Scotland)

## Makars          Scrievers

2008   A C Clarke
2009   Robin Cairns
2010   Maggie Rabatski
2011   Colin Will
2012   Sheila Templeton
2013   Rab Wilson
2014   Anne Connolly
2015   Brian Whittingham
2016   Elizabeth Rimmer
2017   Andy Jackson
2018   Marjorie Lotfi Gill
2019   Stephen Watt          Olga Wojtas
2020   Finola Scott          Charlie Gracie
2021   Jim Mackintosh        Leela Soma
2022   Beth McDonough        Moira McPartlin
2023   Morag Anderson        Carol McKay
2024   Marcas Mac an Tuairneir   Colette Coen

# Foreword

The first section of this volume contains the short stories, flash fiction and poetry of those placed in the Federation of Writers (Scotland) annual Vernal Equinox writing competition for 2023.

*A Playground in Beijing* by James Bradley is the overall winner of the Vernal Equinox competition and recipient of the Brian Whittingham Prize. This award celebrates the life of a former and much loved FWS Makar. The title of the winning piece of writing also becomes the Anthology title.

The following section is of FWS members' writing selected in response to the 2023 anthology call-out.

All pieces of writing included in this year's anthology were submitted anonymously and then selected by invited judges in the case of the Vernal Equinox competition, and in the case of FWS members' writing by the FWS 2023 Scriever, Makar, Scots, and Gaelic conveners. It's satisfying that the process supports inclusion in the anthology based purely on the quality and appeal of each individual's creative work.

Publication in this bi-annual anthology is a fine way to recognise these pieces, to see them preserved in print and shared widely.

Huge thanks and praise go to the FWS committee members, judges, Makar, Scriever, Scots and Gaelic conveners, and – of course – to the writers whose dedication to the craft is celebrated here. A book is far more than flat paper pages. Open it, breathe in, and enjoy!

Carol McKay
2023 Scriever Federation of Writers (Scotland)

# Contents

## Vernal Equinox Competition Winners ........ 1

A Playground in Beijing .................................................................. 2

Blue Garden ..................................................................................... 3

Temporal Shift ................................................................................. 4

Gaoir na Gaoithe ............................................................................. 5

The Screaming Wind ...................................................................... 6

Brot .................................................................................................... 7

Soup ................................................................................................... 8

Cùl-Sleamhnachadh ........................................................................ 9

Back-Sliding ................................................................................... 10

Homework 2040 ........................................................................... 11

Dreich, Dour an Drouthy ............................................................ 13

The Alcomie o Curlin ................................................................. 14

Angie Babe ..................................................................................... 15

My Birds ......................................................................................... 21

Room 12: The Dissection of Anna J, Aged 101 ..................... 26

Tangled up ..................................................................................... 28

Walking with Shadows ................................................................ 30

## Members' writing of the Federation of Writers (Scotland) ..........32

Rootlessness .......................................................................... 33
Anthem .................................................................................. 34
Pylon Pals ............................................................................. 36
Mink ...................................................................................... 38
A Caunle for Chairlie ........................................................... 40
Hand-feeding Birds in Rozelle Park, Ayr ............................. 41
Pacitto's ................................................................................ 42
Rèis Bhun-os-chionn ............................................................ 43
Upside-down Race ................................................................ 44
Future Investments .............................................................. 45
Fruit ...................................................................................... 46
Gairm .................................................................................... 47
A Call .................................................................................... 48
A Sure Place ......................................................................... 49
A Cast for the Numbers ....................................................... 50
The Torrent .......................................................................... 51
Guide to Gaelic Pronunciation (excerpts) ........................... 52
Voices I still hear ................................................................. 54
Visiting Hour ........................................................................ 55
Origins of a Wallflower ........................................................ 56
Birthday Treat ..................................................................... 57
Blame the Dark .................................................................... 58
Reluctant Song ..................................................................... 59
Reservations ......................................................................... 61
Alert ...................................................................................... 62
Edinburgh Festival ............................................................... 63
Scots Word of the Day ......................................................... 64

| | |
|---|---|
| To the Rescue | 65 |
| Sacked | 67 |
| Relaxing by the Pool | 69 |
| Refuge | 70 |
| Coronation Blues | 72 |
| All the Boats | 74 |
| All Day Breakfast in a Tin | 76 |
| Power Cut | 77 |
| Nana and the Jakeys | 78 |
| You Said Aye | 80 |
| Choosing a Book | 82 |
| Old Peaches | 84 |
| Alki | 90 |
| Delivered on a Westerly Wind | 97 |
| Gridlock | 103 |
| The Red Suit | 107 |
| The Walker | 112 |
| Behind the Mirror | 117 |
| Supermarket Starlings | 121 |
| The Gold Bar | 124 |
| A Story of Bones | 126 |

# Vernal Equinox Competition

## Judges

| | | |
|---|---|---|
| Poetry | Morag Anderson | FWS Makar |
| Prose | Carol McKay | FWS Scriever |
| Flash Fiction | Liane McKay | Soor Plooms Press |
| Gàidhlig | Maggie Rabatski | Former FWS Makar |
| Scots | Jo Gilbert | Poet writing in Doric and Scots |

# A Playground in Beijing

On the issue of tattoos
a colleague quoted

Confucius: the body
of the child belongs

to its parents. Extend
this to other figures

of authority.
Outside my window

each school-day
young bodies ordered

for physical routine
in strict geometry.

The grid conflicts
with the chaos of play.

At the back, on the cusp
of supervision

an impious few
disrupt the pattern

with gestures of boredom;
attitudes of rebellion.

**James Bradley**
*Winner of the Brian Whittingham Prize*

# Blue Garden

We are so pleased with it.
Far from a fad,
we have always been mad for blue.

It's nothing new for us.
Our house is awash with blue,
as you will have seen
from the crockery alone
not to mention the statement walls.
Yes, there's always been
this yearning for blue.

This is a garden in the spell
of twilight, a solar eclipse.
It's a boat steady on the blue of glacial melt.
and whatever blue horizon there is
we never wish to go beyond it.

Through these various blooms,
these garnered particulars:
scattered pebbles, sea-smoothed glass,
shards of smashed pots,
we fix the names of blue
and sit for hours in sedated peace,
with no purpose other than to be lulled,

while every evening the moth children gather
at the fence, peeping through the gaps.
The little pipsqueaks
are no trouble at all. They too love blue.
You should see them. Their glee,
their muted laughter,
their tiny, pointed teeth.

**David Mark Williams**
*Highly Commended*

# Temporal Shift
*after Philip Larkin*

Riding backwards on the train,
all that I know falls away.

The future behind me slips
past peripheral vision,

streams to the horizon
turning to rain.

The folk facing forwards—they
think they see what's coming.

**Gillian Dawson**
*Commended*

# Gaoir na Gaoithe

*Ann an dlùth-phàirteachas leis an luchd-iomairt Sàmach, Nirribhidh*

Far an robh tost,
tha a' ghaoth na gaoir,
a' sgapadh an trèid.

Far an robh fàs an fheòir,
a' breacadh an t-sneachda,
a-nis, tha colbh geal

Nach do bhris a-mach
o chlàr na talmhainn,
ach air a chur ann

A dh'aona-ghnothach,
le làmh choigreach, gun
chùram do shruth deò –

Bèist gun anail, neo-
ghluasadach ach le
plumadaich a ghàirdeanan

A dh'innseas briseadh
slighe fèidh-imrich,
bacadh bàir dùthchais.

**Marcas Mac an Tuairneir**
*Winner of the Gaelic poetry prize*

# The Screaming Wind

*In solidarity with the Sami activists, Norway*

Where once was silence,
the wind now screams,
scattering the herd.

Where once grass grew,
speckling the snowfall,
now, a white column

That never erupted
from the earth's crust,
placed there, instead

With purpose, by
alien hand, careless
to the vital flow –

A beast without breath,
motionless, but for
its flailing arms

Speak only of rupture,
blocks reindeer's migration,
a birthright's beaten path.

**Marcas Mac an Tuairneir**

# Brot

Ath-bheothachadh ar slàinte,
air a briseadh le saoghal farsaing,
gar còmhdachadh, tiugh is fàilteachail,
ann am blàths is sàbhailteachd.

Nar n-òige bhiodh i a' plubadaich, gun sgur.
Aon rud fìor – as fhiach a chumail,
pàirt den t-struileag-thillidh
is gach fear is tè dhuinn a' cur ris.

Ar gàrradh, lusan de gach seòrsa,
làn de bhlas sònraichte,
talamh mothachadh ar sinnsearan
gar beartachadh, gar lìonadh.

Eadar sgalan gàire is tuiltean deòir –
chan eil cuimhne far an d' rinneadh a' phoit
a bha gun toiseach, gun chrìch,
ach maireannach gu deò.

Gus an deach an teas air falbh fòidhpe,
is co-thabhartasan a' crìonadh.
A-nis, chan eil air a shiubhal ach blas meatach,
ach ithidh mi i gu briseadh mo latha.

**Ceitidh Campbell**
*Highly Commended Gaelic poetry category*

# Soup

Renews our health
broken by the wider world,
envelops us, thick and welcoming,
in warmth and safety.

In our youth it always bubbled away.
One truth – worth continuing,
part of the tradition of returning,
and every one of us adding to it.

Our garden, plants of every variety,
full of unique flavour,
the land of our ancestors experience
enriches and fills us.

From peals of laughter to floods of tears –
no one remembered when the everlasting pot
without beginning or end
was made

Until the heat went from under it,
contributions lessened.
Now weakened, there is little connection with its taste,
but I will consume it forever.

**Ceitidh Campbell**

# Cùl-Sleamhnachadh

Cho eòlach 's a tha mi air an àite seo
far an coinnich am muir ris an linne,
agus am bàgh a' tionndadh gu gràsmhor
chun nan taighean-solais a-mach air an rubha
a' toirt ar sùil air an fhairge gun sgur.

Ghluais iad aon dhiubh uair
Fad ceud slat tarsaing air a' mhuran.
B'ann anns an àite cheàrr a bha e
Air sgàth's gun robh na sruthan
Air carachadh thar na linntean.

Leum mi fhìn an-aghaidh an t-srutha,
cùl-sleamhnachadh tro na bliadhnaichean mòra,
 gus na làithean-geala mus do thòisich tìm
agus nam shìneadh air an tràigh
ri taobh mo nighinn àlainn mìn.

Seall! Seo an t-àite sònraichte sin:
An sloc am measg dùin-ghainmhich
far an do phòg mi thu a' chiad uair
agus blas na sàl a bh'air do bhilean
cho milis dhomh ri iasmin.

Cha bhi na làithean seo a' tighinn air ais
ach tha iad nam smaointean fad na h-ùine,
gam lionadh's gam chuairteachadh,
nuair a choisicheas mi ri taobh Linne Tatha
agus mo chridhe làn le cianalas.

**Donnchadh MacCàba**
*Commended Gaelic poetry category*

# Back-Sliding

I know this place so well
where the sea meets the firth,
and the bay turns gracefully
to the lighthouses out on the point
drawing our eye to the endless ocean.

They moved one of them once
a hundred yards over the marram grass.
In the wrong place it was
because the currents
had altered over our lifetimes.

I myself leapt against the currents,
back-sliding through the long years,
to the golden days before time began
and lying stretched out on the beach
beside my beautiful gentle girl.

Look! This is that special place:
the hollow amongst the sand-dunes
where I kissed you for the first time
and the taste of the salt sea upon your lips
was as sweet to me as jasmine.

Those days won't be coming back
but they're with me all the time,
filling me and surrounding me,
when I walk beside the Firth of Tay
and my heart full of sad nostalgia.

**Donnchadh MacCàba**

# Homework 2040

granda aye
wir doin' history at school aye
an' ah've tae interview an auld person aye
ah thought o' you aye
is tha' OK aye
thirty years ago wis thi fine-an'-shall crash aye
an' aw thi poor people git poorer aye
an' thi weather went bad aye
an' thi ice meltit aye
an' thi sea git higher aye
an' aw thi animals wir dyin' aye
an' aw thi people knew an' didnae dae anythin' aye
an' there wis plenty o' food aye
an' thi electricity wis oan aw thi time aye
an' everyone had thir ain privit caur aye
an' flew aboot in airplanes like in the photies in thi school aye
an' hid thir ain computers an' phones an' tvs like in teach's display case aye
even thi kids aye
then aw thi big countries fell oot aye

an' aw thi poor people git mair poorer aye
an' thi virus came aye
an' lots o' people died aye
an' scotland an' england fell oot aye
an' aw thi poor people git even mair poorer aye
an' then thir wis thi second virus aye
an' then thi third an' fourth aye
an' half o' aw people died aye
an' maistly thi auld wans aye
an' everythin' stoapt aye
hospitals aye
travel aye
governments aye
money aye
everythin' aye
an' that's why oor village is fortified aye
granda aye

did it huf tae be like this naw

**Stephen Eric Smyth**
*Winner of poetry written in Scots*

# Dreich, Dour an Drouthy

Ye thocht there wis jist twa alane—
*hit's aither dreich or gey dreich.*
A beg tae differ.

Dreich o the dowie dens o Yarrow,
dreich o the glowerin ben
that chills ye tae the marrow,

gray dreich, jist a spitter in the ee,
an thirlin dreich that drouks the skin
tae daise a bodie's banes,

dreich o the haar, that fairs wi the sun
an dreich o the loordie heid,
the nicht afore that bides aa day,
cleuks out yer dingin hairt
lik an Aztec priest.

There's dreich in staundart Southron noo,
a gless hauf empty wather-wird,
aye ower-uised an dowf,

bit Scots dreich bleezes in a makar's saul,
nae dout at aa the tassie's tuim,
the bottle's oot, the wheich's awa.

**David Bleiman**
*Highly commended for poetry written in Scots*

# The Alcomie o Curlin

Fae Ailsa Craig the fundit magma taen
an turnt bi makkars (turns it) intil curlin stanes

On curlin-pownds the watter-fundit frost
turnt intil rinks whaur gemms is wun or losst

The curlers gars thair stanes be stell'd or chap:
the magma sclys athort the watter's tap

Fyre an watter meets but fundit grees:
the curlin some kin-kynd o alcomie

**Hamish Scott**
*Commended for poetry written in Scots*

# Angie Babe

**Fiona Curnow**
*Winner of short story category*

*Angie Babe Come on, come on...Christ, you've been ages.* It crossed my mind to walk up the path an chap that big fucking door. Aye, it did. Every time it did. But naw, I just stand here like an eejit an watch an try no to think about what's going on an walk a bit an wait an watch an walk a bit an wait.

Finally, she comes out, but something's up wi her. Her hair's a messed up. That makes me feel sick, so it does but...aye. Anyway, she's out. She runs past me. I catch a smell o her, the posh perfume, leather, vodka.
'Ange?' I call, curious like.
'Run!' she hisses back at me, pulling on her jacket, running.

We run up the road, past the big houses. Aye, a squeaky clean. Aye, right! She waves at a taxi that's sitting at the Commie. Exhaust fumes an chlorine.

'What is it?' I ask, slumping back on the seat, gasping, sweating.

'Not now. When we're back at the flat, right?' she says, with this weird seriousness.

'We no gonna pick up first?' I mouth at her. 'I'm scratching, like.' I can feel my eyes staring at her wi their strung-out-an-desperate thing. I wipe my shaking, clammy hands on my jeans. She gives me this stare that says *shut up*, so I do.

We're zipping down Leith Walk. Posh pawn shops an dirty tenements, screaming weans an smoking mums, drunk dads an junkie bums, aye. Home. We get out at the Superstore; the route we usually take when we're carrying. Inconspicuous, like. Blend in wi the shoppers. Next hoof it, as casually as hoofing can be done, down to our bit. No the swanky bit o Leith wi the trendy warehouse conversions. Posh accents an poncie cars, coffee shops an pricey bars. Naw, no there. The other way.

The tenement stinks o piss an puke tinged wi dog shite, but home's home, aye? The old guy from the top floor's passed out beside our door. A can o Special Brew clenched in his grime covered, purple hands. Ange kicks him out the way. He grunts, toppling over on the cold stone floor. I want to stop an check, like, but she drags me in by my sleeve.

'What's going on Ange?' I ask, as she locks all three mortices an slides the two bolts.

'Fuck's sake, man. Fuck's sake!' she breathes, all exasperated like, as she slips ever so slowly down the wall. I've seen her legless often enough but no like this. Naw, no like this at all. Then she starts laughing an crying all together like she's just lost it.

'Ange... Babe. I'm cracking up here. I need a score. Come on will ye? Get it together, doll.' I've got my hands tight on her shoulders an I'm shaking her, shaking her, shaking the crazies out o her. She looks at me, her head cocked to one side. It stabs me. I stop. She tips her shoulder-bag upside down an everything tumbles out on the manky carpet. Her hairbrush, lipstick, dirty knickers, fags, lighter, blade, works, an a Habitat bag sit there. She laughs an shakes it. 'What a tosser!'

"That's no what I think it is, is it?' I ask, shaking so bad I cannae focus, feeling sick, sweating like shit. 'Christ Ange,' I says, clawing at my hair, an I'm off to the kitchen for a spoon.' There's none clean so I wipe the gunk off o one wi my sleeve an head to the table. She's already there laying the packs out. Like bricks wrapped in plastic. It's like they're dancing about, messin wi me. She slices one open wi her blade, sticks her finger in an tastes it. 'Straight from Paki-fuckin-stan. It's not even been cut yet,' she says, like she's just had the best fuck ever. 'Go and do it for me, babes? There's a pal, eh?'

She watches as I boil it up in the spoon. She watches as it bubbles. She watches as I draw it into the needle. She's got the belt pulled tight round her arm. I tap at her veins. They're fucked.

'Your leg, Ange. Let's try your leg, eh?'

I manage. Just. I watch as her eyes go. I fucking love that. Knowing she's got there, that she feels good. I love her that much. I do my hit an we lay there, gouching out for a bit.

'So, are you gonna tell me, or what?' I ask, feeling almost human in that in between hits, life goes on, kinda way.

'I didn't mean it, I swear I didn't,' she says, greetin.

'You didnae mean what? Jesus Ange, there's a fuckin lottery's worth o smack sitting there. Are we in the shit or what?'

'I dunno. Christ,' she says. She scratches at her bare leg wi dirty, stained nails. Flecks o reddish brown mix wi the freckles on her pale, pale skin. She sniffs hard an flicks her head back so as her eyes meet mine.

'He was hurting me real bad. I told him to stop but he wouldn't. He just kept on...hurting me.'

'Aw Christ, Ange...I didnae know.' I'm the one greetin now, feeling like shite. She comes an wraps herself around me. Her legs an arms an hair, everything. An I'm swimming in her an I love it an I hate it, a mixed up. I push her hair behind her ears. She's dyed it again. No need. 'You're gorgeous Ange. So fucking gorgeous. You know that, aye?'

'So you keep telling me,' she whispers, right close, in my ear, so that I can feel the words. She wipes her nose wi the back o her hand, like a wee kid.

'We need to stop this, Ange,' I says, stroking her arm, no looking at her. 'It's so fucked up an I let you do that shit cos I'm a fuckin junkie, eh?' I look at her now. 'What kinda shit's that?'

She smiles. 'Yeah. Yeah, we do. We can sell it, yeah? Get ourselves into a posh rehab? Get straight? Yeah?' She's looking all excited now, like she's been dusted. 'Maybe even get the kid back, eh?'

'Aye, maybe,' I says, but I'm thinking, no that again. The wean's gone Ange. 'How did you get it?' I says. 'The gear?'

'I was in the bathroom, cleaning myself up. Blood and...,' she pauses an thinks for a bit. I dinnae want to know what's in her head.

'Piece of shit,' she spits. 'Anyway, my stomach was hurting real bad, and I sort of stumbled and then this panel popped out of the wall, like. Then I saw the bag. I didn't know what it was, like. I thought maybe money, yeah? Didn't know the guy was a dealer.' She looks up at me for confirmation. I nod. 'Anyway, I pulled it out, stuffed it in my bag and pretended like nothing had happened.' She shrugs. Story over.

'You know he'll be after you?' I says, trying to get it right. 'We need to get out o here.'

'Yeah, but...'

'Naw. We need to move, Babe. The man's a thug.'

'Yeah, but, he's...dead.' She does that laugh cry thing again. 'I–stabbed–him,' she manages to get out between the fucked-up noise she's making. She takes a deep breath an drills her eyes right into me. 'Killed the bastard,' she says, as if – I dunno – as if it was okay.

I feel like the blood's been drained out o me. I cannae breathe. 'Naw, Angie Babe. Naw.'

Another hit. Block it out. Get it together. An we're hoofing it again. Thank fuck, the old geezer's gone. Just a stain left. We jump on a bus heading to Davie's place at Marchmont. We go upstairs. It's full o schoolies making loads o noise, taking the piss. That's good. They're getting a the tuts an stares. The stench o chips an pies churns my stomach. They pile out on Princes Street. Silence. Finally we get there. 'Cheers, mate,' I says to the driver.

I gie Ange a hug as I press the shiny brass buzzer.

'Okay, Babe?' I ask.

She smiles.

The door clicks open an up we go. I get right down to business an show him what we've got.

He whistles, a long, drawn out, fuck-me type whistle. 'I can shift it, mate, for sure, but...I ain't got that kind of cash, you know?'

'Naw. Understand, Davie man. Course. We just need a bit the now. The rest later's fine, aye?' 'I'm guessing you're in bother here?' he says.

I shrug. 'Aye, a wee bit,' I says, trying to be casual but letting him know. Keeping it straight.

'How much can you get hold o the now, like?'

'Twenty grand?'

'That would be fucking brilliant!' I can feel what's going on in her head, feel the relief. 'Right. You two sit tight, okay? I'll be right back.'

An he's gone.

'Shit,' she says, as she sits down an strokes the velvet cushions of his settee. 'Is this for real? I mean can you trust the guy, yeah?'

'Aye, nae bother. We go way back, him an me. He's sound,' I says, as I'm looking out the window, checking the street. We're at Waverley station waiting on a train.

'Christ, there's coppers everywhere,' Ange whispers.

'We're fine,' I says. 'Just ignore them like normal, aye? We're no carrying. It's fine.' I squeeze her waist.

'Well,' she says, looking at me a sheepish, like.

'What?'

'Nothing,' she says, turning away, following the clatter o some posh bags skipping along the concrete, off on a nice wee holiday. We're standing there, staring up at the departures as they flicker an wink, giving us the come-on like a slapper at a disco. We dinnae take our eyes off o it. Your new life's about to depart from platform...Aye.

'That's it,' she says, all excited. 'Platform two, see?' she points up at the board. I smile cos it's cute. The wee girl in her. We make for the platform, purposeful, heads down. No like we used to when we were here lifting. Eyes peeled, scanning. Foreigners wi loud mouths an fat wallets, vacant looks an bulging pockets. Aye, easy pickings. Careful, mind. Polis everywhere, cameras too, spying on you. Sneaky cunts!

'I can't believe we're doing this. We're really doing it. Christ,' she says. Her lips are smiling, but I can see in her eyes she's scared.

'I know, eh? Seven hours then rehab. Shit. ' I shake my head an laugh. 'Wonder what it'll be like?

'The place? Should be nice eh? At that price!'

'Yeah,' she says, looking at me a guilty, like. 'Look, I've brought a wee packet. Just enough for one last wee hit each. For the journey, yeah?'

'Christ. I thought we were clean,' I says, disappointed, but kinda relieved too.

'I'll just go now, eh? Just a toot, not a fix. You can go after, right?'

'Aye, right. No works though. Just a toot. Promise?'

'Yeah, sure,' she smiles an heads off to the toilets.

I'm looking up at the engaged sign then out the window at the blur o somewhere else, the sign, the blur, the sign, the blur. Too long. She's taking too fucking long. My stomach shrinks, my head thumps, I cannae breath. I force my legs to work. The noises swarm together. Bits o conversation, the screech o the train, the buzzing in my head. I reach the toilet an chap the door, quiet like. 'Ange,' I whisper. 'Ange.' I chap louder but I dinnae want to. I know. I can feel it. Like she's been torn out o me. The guard says something. I cannae hear him. He opens the door. I see the needle. I see the eyes, staring. Cold. Vacant. *Naw. Naw, Angie Babe. What am I gonna do now, eh? What the fuck am I gonna do now?*

# My Birds

**Claire Demenez**
*Commended in the short story category*

When I regained consciousness, I was feeling nothing but atrocious pain below my right knee. I had the suffocating sense of being immobilised, the crystal-clear awareness that no muscle of mine would want to move. After the pain, my first coherent thought was that it might subdue very soon, so long as I remained paralysed and unable to make it any worse. I closed my eyes again and focused on the idea that my mind would acclimatise and ease into whatever predicament I'd found myself in. I could tell I was under a lot of pressure.

I tried to puzzle together what might have happened from the memories I could conjure. It had been morning, I had been out of bed. Yes, I'd been making coffee in the kitchen, staring down at the percolator, unsure what else to do with myself until the drink was ready. I remembered the sputtering sounds of hot coffee rising just as the pendant light began to sway. Then it all came back to me: the shaking feet of my only kitchen chair and tiny round table, the clinking of the glassware on the drying rack, and finally, the vacillating bookshelf's shadow pouncing over me.

I could tell I was sandwiched somewhere in the middle of a pile of detritus. I thought I could smell the lingering aroma of my spilled coffee, although this might have only been my brain filling gaps in logic for me. I could see nothing nor move my neck, but I could feel the overall pressure was lighter against the skin of my left cheek. I hadn't noticed it at first, what with the intense pain in my leg. As my senses continued to return, I heard a chirp followed by the fluttering sound of feathers in motion. What was digging into my cheek was the wiry frame of my birdcage. At least one of my canaries must still be alive.

I always placed the cage on my kitchen table before making my morning coffee, so it only made sense it would have fallen near, or over, me. My two birds insisted that I attend to them as soon as I woke up and would not tolerate being taken out of the kitchen while I had breakfast. In fact, I usually carried the cage around the house with me, unable to bear the heart-wrenching cries that would emanate from its occupants if I left their line of sight. I reasoned that there was a high chance both birds had survived. Otherwise, I'd be feeling the weight of a dead body limp against my cheek.

I heard familiar footsteps scrambling my way. Then a thud, perhaps of an ass lowered onto the pile.

'Son, is that you under there?'

'Dad, it's you. Yes dad, here I am. Right beneath you. All trapped.'

'Well don't you move just now. Let me have a look. Oh son, that's your whole house down, isn't it? Let's see what we can do.'

My father sits above my house, above me, the rubble, and the small pocket of air carved out by the birdcage against my face. I think he's crying. I can hear him sifting through the shallower layers of broken tiles and splintered wooden pillars, sometimes stopping perhaps to examine something he's excavated. I can feel his weight shifting around the structure and brace myself for more pain and crushing. But I can't see myself telling him to stop, to stop looking for my things.

The birds and the cage were a gift from my father. He'd arrived at my house one day, shortly after I moved in, for no particular reason. The cage was covered in taped-up newspaper pages, not the ones he usually read, with a few finger-sized holes poked straight through the top. It wasn't hard to guess what was inside, although I hadn't expected the birds to come in a pair. He'd said it was so they could keep each other company. So, I wouldn't be too preoccupied with them when I was away. Both could have fit in the palm of my hand. They looked like feathery egg yolks, bouncing from perch to perch, engrossed in a weightless mutual chase.

I imagine him holding what he finds. Maybe trying to piece together shards of my favourite CD or dusting off the little booklet with all the lyrics inside. Or delicately bringing to his face a loose handle, chipped off of my favourite mug, pretending to drink from it. Maybe he's tugging at a dirty tea towel and examining the stains, assessing which ones were made by the collapse of my house and which ones come from an attempt at reducing tomato sauce.

I wait patiently, let my mind run free fuelled by the sounds of him. The pain returns but nothing around me has moved. The nerves along my leg pulse relentlessly as they shoot more and more pain signals through to my spine, as if they want to share it, to diffuse it, not to be the only limb sustaining that much damage. I feel each one of them being pulled out of my flesh and lashed back into it. I wait for it to pass, for my dad to return. My eyes are closed, and I know all I can do is breathe through the waves. When an animal is in too much pain it just gets put down. But my poor father is watching me suffer with dignity, keeping it together is only the most meagre form of kindnesses I could return.

I feel a sticky wetness spreading over my face. Bird droppings. I suppose they can still fly to their feeder, maybe they even have a bit of water left in the miniature cistern I bolted to the sidings. I wish I could move my hand and wiggle my fingers through the wire to wipe it off my face. I probably could, in fact. Focussing on the warm liquid seems to cake over the painful sensations in my leg. I can feel my fingers wiggling and I press my thumb against the pads of my other digits. But I'm scared of endangering the structure of the pile. I don't want it all to collapse over me or reawaken my leg.

My dad doesn't reach down to wipe the shite off me. I don't ask him to dig me out either. I figured if he didn't offer, the pile must look too precarious or daunting. If it was doable, he would have done it. I know that to be true about my father.

'That's one thing I've always admired in you. That sense of calm. Even now you're not freaking out.'

I can sense a tinge of emotionality in my father's voice. Pride laced with worry. I think he's trying to reassure me, to encourage me. I've got this. I'll be fine.

'Thanks dad. I'm sure someone will come and get me out soon.'

'Maybe if you rest a bit longer you'll gather the strength to crawl out.'

'I think my leg's broken, dad. Could you go check if someone's coming to help me?'

'I can't leave you alone, son. We can wait together; someone will come for sure.'

I think of my father, all the way back to the day he drove me to this house, my very own house. I had a few boxes piled in the boot that would drift left or right with the curving of the road. I think that day he'd let me play that favourite CD of mine. My dad always enjoyed his car. From a very young age he let me ride in the passenger seat, propped up on a cushion until I grew big enough to see above the dashboard, and whenever he had to break sharply his arm instinctively stretched over my chest to protect me. After I learned to drive, I realised this would never have worked in a real crash.

I can hear movement around me, other animals smaller than me scurrying through the mess. I wish my body could shrink twenty-fold. The pocket of air would be so wide. But no doubt I would immediately be crushed by the gigantic birdcage falling over me. As for my poor birds, they're already just as small as the mice and insects. The bars around them are tighter than my loose blanket of beams and tiles. They could shrink all they want, there's no chance they could squeeze out.

'You know son, I think the door to that cage is facing up. If it's not too bent out of shape, I might be able to open it. How about we give this pair a chance?'

My dad speaks as if he'd been privy to my inner thoughts. I hear his fingers come closer as he reaches into the hole in the rubble, and when they reach the cage, the clinkering of his fingernails dragging over the metal wire for the hook of the door.

'But dad, won't they die in the wild? You know they cry if I don't feed them before myself every morning?' I am growing agitated at my dad's clumsy attempt to help them. I don't think they're fit for life outside of the cage. I've already lost my house; I can't have them fly away now.

'Just trust me, son. I wouldn't do it if I wasn't confident about this.'

The rusty hinges of the door creak and I hear the birds' wings flap with excitement.

'Son, you should see this. They're just waiting outside the cage. I think they still want you to take care of them.'

I'm too tired to speak to him.

'Right, let me get them down to my car. I've got an old shoebox they can stay in for now, until you get out. You just stay still.'

I could hear less and less of my father's words as he moved away, as the friction of his rubber shoes on the broken shards of concrete covered his voice. Perhaps I even imagined that a last few words of care were swallowed up between the sounds of my crumbled house.

It was a few hours until footsteps returned. The rescuers must have come in a group of five, maybe six. The collapsed structure was so entangled with my own I hardly felt the weight of their bodies and tools. A face peered into my hole and asked how long I'd been there. When I said I wasn't sure, I wondered if he would leave and ask my father, but to my surprise the rescuer continued:

'It must have been tough waiting so long on your own. I think you might have fainted and lost track of time. It's been a full day since the earthquake. Your neighbours said they thought you were out visiting family, it's only when they saw your wee birds fly out that they realised you might have been trapped under with them and called us. Lucky you! Life saved by your pets, happens more often than you'd think. It was good of you to set them free.'

He stayed there, lying by my side, and described the cranes and the orderly manoeuvres that were being conducted around me as the digging got underway. Perfectly still while his colleagues were lifting my house's torn cypress beams, its shattered brick tiles, its countless pieces of crumbled concrete. His hand reached down to feel my face and rubbed a wet wipe against the crusty droppings, careful to get it all off. Hours passed and I drifted in and out consciousness, exhausted, until I smelled someone bringing him a paper cup full of coffee.

'Would you like a sip,' he asked, and before I could reply he lowered the cup down into the cage, tipped it against one of the metal bars, and let the hot drink dribble slowly along my cheek down to my lips.

# Room 12: The Dissection of Anna J, Aged 101

**Harry MacDonald**
*Winner of the Flash Fiction category*

Oh, it was something. A *Y* incision worthy of its own font. We peeled back the history of a life. Respectful, careful, like archaeologists. Dendrochronologists. We shone a light, drew a breath. Marvelled at what we saw.

We found windswept meadows spattered with wild flowers, busy with life, rainbow hued. Buttercups and dandelions ablaze like mini suns; bluebells and thistles. Forget-me-nots that still remembered. A walk in the heather, a first walk, hand in hand with the boy next door.
Love: that knew no compass but the heart.

We went forward as explorers. Some time in her past she'd swallowed an ocean, for we found one. Foaming like a mad thing, breaking on rocks, black and gnarled, that clawed at the sand. An island. Where she'd swam naked with a castaway named Olsen. Who'd taught her how to swear in Swedish, how to climb mountains whose magnificence took her breath away, and ours. In the end all she left him was a broken heart and a treasure map.

Cutting our way further in, where the light hardly ever reaches, we found a whole forest of pines. Ten-day stubble on a great jawline of a hillside. Where once-upon-a-time Anna walked with her children, skipping over branches and roots. Collecting; naming creepy-crawlies; giving made-up names to trees where time had torn a face. Gathering pine cones and caterpillar coats as treasure. Children that she'd outlived. Loved. Sorrows she'd tasted that she was never meant to know.

Inside Anna J we discovered landscape and seascape, as she had, vista after vista, stretching into the past. Constellations she'd charted her life by. Wild places that had changed her and she'd left unchanged. Deserts where sand had snuck inside her boots and singed her eyes to make her cry: not for any other reason. Lines of sugar frosted peaks that ricocheted against the sky the way her heart bounded at every new horizon.

Nearby in her anatomy, out of time, we found a house on a rain-black street.

A small attic room on the *Left Bank*, four floors up on *Rue de Savoie* in Paris; simple, scant; a defiant cactus plant framed in the window. A place where she'd once spent time with a famous artist. But they'd clashed, often, like the place where the sea meets the land. He praised her warmth, the way her mouth naturally inclined to a smile; he loved her light that illuminated the possible; and caused her hair to lighten to the gold of wheat. But he cursed her fire that burned too intense. *Demaisado!* The gods were bound to notice. She called him a crazy old Spaniard.

Until, one day, she left him, and us, a note pinned to the inside of the door, not visible from the outside:

*For the benefit of all. One carefree owner. Gone travelling. Anna J.*

# Tangled up

**Tracy Geddes**
*Highly commended in the Flash Fiction category*

It felt like my mam had fallen backwards into a pond. Deeper and deeper. Just beyond my fingertips.

Her lovely clothes get torn then a jelly fish stings her. Shock. My mam doesn't seem to even notice. Further still she sinks, splitting her head open on a rock, blood floating. Christ almighty, that's it. I plunge in after her.

"Mam, your head" I scream. She is twirling and descending.
She replies "It wis the woman that moved into my loft. I telt her get the hell oot of my hoose and her man came doon and hit me on the head."
Tragically predictable by this time. As is my reply. "Mam, there canna be folk living in your loft."

Seaweed tangling round my limbs, like slippery hands. We descend, colder and deeper and darker, into open sea. Her handbag floats past, flowery phone case, purse and money, bingo cards, store cards, lipstick and eyeliner, then little cards saying cooking, counting, sewing, then dignity, pride, rationale and finally, her house keys, floating away and snapped up by a predator while her whole life cards lie weeping with the whelks.

My lungs are bursting. I ascend, breathe and away back down. Through the tangles, desperately searching. The motion and crashing tricks my vision. I'm caught again, hostage of the grabbing hands. She's there but, wait, she's not alone. She's smiling, but It's not me she's smiling at. The sea stills and I see the serpent. Circling my mam. A thick head of silver hair, shirt and tie, tidy trousers and he's smiling his serpent smile at my mam. Oh-oh. Oh no.

"Mam!" I say sharply. She looks round but then, smiling up at him says "will you be my boyfriend?"

Vision wavy but I make out letters D-E-M-O-N along the back of his jacket. They're dancing now. He's been a sympathetic ear. The serpent turns to me but, instead of a face, there's nothing but a black hole. I recoil in horror and am fighting to free myself. The serpent is coming. I cannot breathe. He points and I'm tumbling over and over backwards. I surface.

I plead "can somebody please help my mam?" Nobody can. Some have empathy. They know. Down again I dive. No sign but I hear the beautiful strains of John Lennon's 'Woman' from every direction. My mam's terrified of water. Armbands aged 55. Won't go out in the rain in case it spoils her hair. I'm carried by the swell. Smashed against rocks, I see her. Her blonde hairdo is grey, and her face is bruised. A shape shifts. It's him. His jacket is hung up and I see the whole word now. D-E-M-E-N-T-I A. He's a shark. He starts to eat one of her legs. She's still smiling as he's devouring her. My lungs. I have to let go. I have bairns. I surface and gasp. A breaking wave carries me in.

# Walking with Shadows

**Lesley Traynor**
*Commended in the Flash Fiction category*

Aged ten, I accepted some facts. First, I loved mountains and second, I knew that my granny was dead and that it was pointless for my father to visit her in hospital.

It wasn't my father's reaction that disturbed me, although spectacular, it was my mother's silence when she looked at me. As if something had been confirmed.

'Maybe you should phone and check?' She quietly suggested to him.

His return from the hospital brought grief into the house. My mother packed my words away into the same place she deposited all life's disturbances.

I was twenty when she casually mentioned friends had organised a visit to a *Spey wife*, a clairvoyant.

'We need you to drive us.' She stood in her blue wool coat, handbag over her arm.

'Fine, but I stay in the car.'

I parked up next to a yellow picket fence, my passengers huddled on the pavement garnering strength for the journey up the short path. My mother argued with me, 'it's too cold to sit out here for hours.' She placed me in the advance guard and forced me into the beige of the hallway.

Sharp turquoise eyes blazed in delight. 'I'll take you first, hen.'

Oh, my mother's smirk showed this had been planned.

The *Spey wife* was tiny and squat. A sparrow in an armchair fluffing a woollen shawl around herself. Winter lived in her front room. A child's hand waved me into a chair directly opposite.

'You have it. As strong as me, maybe stronger.'

I squirmed.

'They're here, standing just there.'

I turned to my right.

'They usually walk next to you. But you know that, don't you, hen. They protect you. And you'll be needing them where you're going.'

A vivid description of a strange place followed. A fantastical location high in the mountains where houses were constructed of rubbish. Danger surrounded me but I would be safe. Protected by the shadows beside me I assumed. I let her ravings exhaust her.

She abruptly changed to describe the present.

'And there's a wee collie dug sitting at the feet of the woman beside you.'

I half listened, and wondered how long she would keep up the nonsense.

'The poor woman was young when she passed over. She's holding her arm with the pain.'

The others glared at me when I finally returned and announced the next person was to go in. Let them experience sitting in a fridge for half an hour.

'Well?' My mother asked.

'It was freezing, and she talked nonsense. About living up a mountain in a hot country. So, definitely not Scotland.'

'She must have said something interesting. You were in for long enough.'

I told her about the woman with the dog.

'My mother. She died when I was twenty. Breast cancer. You have her eyes.'

Ethiopia is a war zone. In the mountains, locals construct homes from debris. I turn, smile at my granny.

# Members' writing of the Federation of Writers (Scotland)

*selected by*

Makar, *Morag Anderson*
Scriever, *Carol McKay*
Gàidhlig convener, *Marcas Mac an Tuairneir*
Scots convener, *Ann MacKinnon*

# Rootlessness

### Shasta Hanif Ali

*- somewhere between Pakistan & Scotland*

I long to find the tree you sat under as a child,
candlelight ebbing and flowing; chalk over slate
perfecting the curved strokes of a language
—I dared lose.

I long to find the tree you sat under as a child,
sit with my spine furrowed into trunk,
eat Pakistani sweet mangoes & berries plucked fresh
—sink into the earth that mothered you     but not me.

I dream to walk barefoot over ancestral lands,
swim like you did in the turquoise waters so clear
—I see my reflection in an ice-cold loch

                      a quine stares back aw' hazel eyed,
              haar wrapping its cauld fingers aroond her,
   an atlas veined across her skin   but nae place to point hame
  —her cinnamon pelt hangs in a vitrine labelled: *a selkie acquired.*

I long to find the tree you sat under as a child,
trace each knotted dua into bark: deodar to pine,
—unearth my grief laden body to soil: to seed.

The motherland gathers clay—soul—dust,
whispers in the language of remembering
—*beti, it was his kismet to uproot homelands to homes*
                                    *in new lands.*

*dua* - prayer
*beti* - daughter
*kismet* – fate

# Anthem

**Anne Pia**

And the birds didnae sing,
doon there,
amang the deid steps o marchin,
amang the greetin masses,
standing fer oors, a' nicht,
waitin' tae bow an pass an English Queen.


But mibbae they did i' her lovit glens,
an mibbae they sang at the freshness;
an' the sicht o a new sun;
chantin' ther tunes
at the shy dancing o mists come a' too early;
fa'in saft,  an merry-like,
on glib watters an' the rocks o anither story;
paintin' the moor an' featherin' the heather;
joyful notes
at it a' finally ower;
an dun weel they telt us.

Nae burds nor sangs i' our cities neether;
at her lang slau passin'
an us, wheeshed an solemn.
But twas oor mammies and wer auld yins we saw;
an' we touched again
the erst warm hands o' ancestors.

Then, frae somewhere high up,
ayont rafters and tale turrets
o' castles, keeps and closes,
furth the stirring fields, Fife's Kingdom,
aye, o' Glenfinnan too,
no yin,
but a crowd o' saltires,
flappin' an wavin' they wur;
an'oor cheering herts in proud tune wi' the burds,
wi' a shiverin' reed,
the steady, thrum
o' a singel piper;
an' independence's
long lost anthem.

# Pylon Pals

**Morag Smith**

nnnnnn,,,bzzzzp

    Y'alright there?

wit, whit, t,t,t,t,t

    Take it easy, wi aw get the jitters
    when we're first connected – s'lovely here
    - forest, flowers, a burn, and see that sign?
    Yer in a newt sanctuary! Though
    I've seen none since they fixed the drainage
    - ah might have fried a few by accident.

nnnewtzzzzzz

    S'not ma fault is it? They should've read
    that letter they stuck on the lampposts,
    "network improvements", which means you
    and no more marsh; you're in luck though,
    you've got me to set you right
    and clarify your existential purpose.

exs…nnnzzzz???

    We are the conduits, the A team,
    there's ninety thousand of us, all those cables
    criss-crossed in the sky; when it's windy
    we sing together through the teatime surges;
    did you know, poets started a movement
    just for us, 'cos we're cool and built
    to survive storms, floods, extinctions…

exst,t,t....nnnnnnnn???

        Dinnae stress, take the long view;
        the numpties that put us here
        willnae last, but we will stand
        poised on this horizon – I'm thinking
        post-apocalyptic solarpunk
        icons, dripping moss and ivy, jammed
        with starling nests, tenth generation
        amphibians tickling our capacitors.

nnnewtzzzz!
        At the very least amigo - this
        is only oor first life.
        Now, feel the power.

# Mink

**Stephen Watt**

Just another disposable word
propelled in the playground.

Not like *you* had feelings. Bully.
Cracked knuckles, abraded on bedroom walls,
threatening others for lunch money.

You slept in class a lot. A spurned theatre wig
lying atop folded arms, thwacked
awake by a plastic ruler.
Then language
which no alphabet bunting
had ever taught us before.

We believed you were in detention
when we gazed back into the classroom
through the grubby glass.
In truth, the heat of one flaxen bulb
echoed goldfinches flapping
in a wildflower meadow

compared to the numbing shadows
and inhospitable apparitions
of your home.

I had complained about your smell.
The lapsed onion of your jumper
or congested funk of your barnet
when forced to sit next to one another.

*Now* –
I look up at the light
which is left on in your childhood bedroom
each of your birthdays,

and I think about your mother,
                        arms speckled
like a loveliness of harlequin ladybirds
measuring her infinite guilt
in milliliters.

# A Caunle for Chairlie

**Gordon D. W. Scott**

Hauf an oor afore A meet
the ithers aheid o the sun
tae pit up a wird ower zoom
A licht yer caunle, no sure if A still dae it
for the mindin o ye or fae habit,
like tappin the gless or feedin the dug.
Still and aw, A howp yon ither place is real
and that you war safely gaithert in,
for wan day A'd present masel:
the secont go at a secont son.
Wha dee'd so's A could live?
No Jesus, but you, still-born Chairlie,
ma faur-aff aulder long-lost brither,
A'm the wan for wha ye dee'd
and in whose steid A got tae live.

# Hand-feeding Birds in Rozelle Park, Ayr

**Damaris West**

Don't speak, or move
your hand, or stare
although your eye rejoices
in red breast, blue cap,
white cheek.
They're wary in their
dinosaur brains
of any sparkle of intent.
You'll feel the pressure
of their perch (is this
what reading Braille
is like?) but not
their peck as they select
the coconut from your display
of cereal.

How many seasons
of trust
are you inheriting?
How many cruelties
would it require to undermine
this beautiful
exchange of sustenance?

# Pacitto's

**Jane Lamb**

Today the seagulls and the wind in the city
blew me back to the front at Redcar
where we fought what you called a sea breeze,
but I said was gale force and Baltic.
You told me the ice cream parlour was a local Mecca.
Families came from Teesside on the train
to paddle and play on the beach and then
eat "lemon tops" at Pacitto's.

We ordered at the Formica counter
and sat looking out on the bleak promenade
watching the spray rising as the waves of high tide
splattered against the sea wall.
You were remembering your trips there,
the treat of escaping the fug of Middlesbrough
with your father in his weekend shirt and no tie
and your mother in a good mood,
taken back to her youth
by the sweet and sour treat.

# Rèis Bhun-os-chionn

**Ceitidh Campbell**

gach latha 's mi feitheamh
mo rèis làitheil a ruith
gunna-tòiseachaidh na maidne
nì fuasgladh mo strì
riaghailtean rin leantainn
air aon dòigh na lire.
cumam an cearcall ceart,
gus ruith mar an ceudna
eadar na loidhnichean geala,
gun leigeil corra-bhùthag às
sùil na h-iolaire gam sgrùdadh
airson mearachdan.
leanam an luchd-ceuma,
cumam suas riutha,
a' feuchainn gun tarraing aire,
a' cur cas às dèidh coise.
gheibh mi buinnig
ach
aig a' cheann thall
cha toil leam ruith.

# Upside-down Race

**Ceitidh Campbell**

every day I'm waiting
to run my daily race.
a morning starter gun -
to release my struggle.
rules to follow
like the rest of the pack.
keep the circle correct,
run like the others.
between the white lines,
don't allow a toe-tip out.
hawkeye is watching
for my mistakes.
follow the pacemakers,
and keep up with them,
try not to draw attention,
put one foot in front of the other.
I will win
but
at the end of the day
I don't like running.

# Future Investments

**Jim Aitken**

The turbulence happened
when the money melted away,
fell into the ocean like giant icebergs
making sea levels rise
and threatening floods of despair.

The jitters came along next
when a speculation of traders
and a sensation of journalists
got nations to cut their spending
on non-essential things like health
and housing, education, and the rest
with the sole exception of their wars
and there was some disquiet about this.

The confidence would only return
said the speculation and the sensation
when there were no wars left to fight,
the poor, malnourished and homeless
along with those swelling the jails
had all died off as they should
and they could then invest in thin air
making the markets buoyant once more.

# Fruit

**Ian McDonough**

An idea fell
out of my mind
like a dead squirrel
from a tree.

Its bounciness was high
and it took some time
to come to rest
among its brothers and sisters
on the schoolroom floor.

Our teacher asked
If the river was ten yards wide
and clouds were green
how many eggs would John have?

But I was looking
at Mary-Ann McInness
in an entirely new way.

# Gairm

**Victoria Maciver**

Cha robh a dhìth ach aon cheum
Coltach ri Alice tron *Looking Glass*
Bidh e a' gairm ormsa, saoghal eile
Ach faid analach air falbh

Bidh craobhan còmhdaichte
Le meirge a' caoineadh
Air slighean òir lùbach
Leacaichte ann an làraichean
An dà chuid sean agus ùr
A' cur dol a rannsachadh romham.

Nì mi mo sheasamh mar fhreumhan san ùir
Ged a tha draghan a' falbh leis a' ghaoith
An dùil ri tilleadh
Mar a bhios na ràithean a' dol seachad

Tha mo chridhe ag èirigh mar a' chroman
Dannsa ann an cearcallan gu h-àrd
Mo chasan ghoirt dham thilleadh
Chun toisich
Mar òran a luchdadh a-nuas

# A Call

**Victoria Maciver**

It took but a single step
Like Alice through the Looking Glass
It calls to me, another world
But a breath away

Rust covered trees weep
Onto winding gold paths
Paved in prints both ancient and new
Beckoning me to explore

I ground myself like roots to soil
Whilst worries wash away in the wind
Destined to return like the seasons pass

My heart soars like the kite
Dancing in circles above
My aching legs return me
To the beginning
Like a song on download

Although I depart I leave something
Of myself here or perhaps take it
With me,
Unseen like a missing jigsaw piece

A feeling,
Of hope

# A Sure Place
*In memoriam Aonghas (Dubh) MacNeacail*

**David Betteridge**

Black as the raven is,
so was the young Aonghas,
famously, in beard and mane;
            thereafter,
he morphed to the colour
of granite, most durable of stone;
        thence,
by slow degrees, to the semblance
of doves and clouds,
   until
he was as the snow is,
in the sun's gleam;
          but always,
through every turn and phase
of his life's maturing, there ran
and ran the same strong stem
of a great force.

Beautifully, it blossomed,
again and again,
as deep song.

He has crossed now
from this world's vagaries
to a sure place in our remembering
and our honouring.

There, where his words' sap
renews,
    and the tongue that he graced
        endures,
 there, enjoying the heights
             he will soar with ravens
and doves, and with larks
               ascending.

# A Cast for the Numbers

**Donald Saunders**

I walked a long trail
to cast a light line.

Crouching on the shore
of Loch an Easain
as trout rises dimpled and ringed
the bay in the milky dawn,
I tied on leader and tippet
and the patterns for the morning:

> For the tail fly,
> crow black of shelving depths,
> tinsel of surface shimmer
> or twitching fry,
> tail tag a rowan berry.

> For the dropper,
> a spider hackle, reddish
> speckle of gravelly shallows,
> green-bronze herl of water weed,
> sand, sedges, sphagnum moss.

> On the bob, a
> bristle of heathery banks,
> gold flecks of tormentil
> and a flash of summer sky
> from a blue jay's wing.

Trudging home at sundown,
my catch landed,
all the bright lochans
in the woven creel of memory.

* 'The numbers' is local name for a chain of lochs between Foinaven and Ben Arkle, Sutherland.

# The Torrent

### Karen Hodgson Pryce

*Glenfeshie 1830-35 by Edwin Landseer*

The glacier melted moments before:
the chisel of its shrink unsung.
A slight
thrummed by the dissolving sun
in the trees or the tarred shadows
spilling
the hills. Like an old friend having
travelled far to pay her respects.

From the smooth cortege you make
a mental note to thank her, but
the man behind
the bar wants paying and someone's
daughter has knocked a glass.
By the time
you reach for the long-forgotten,
the room is stark of it.

So you turn back to the valley
where an ocean could surge through
at any time. Nothing
in its torrent but one small lodge:
not even a boot to sandbag the past.

Only a gentle yielding to come
what was. Its occupants assume
the daily routine:
tending the fire, sweeping
the stone floor, seasoning the fowl.
And forgiving themselves.

# Guide to Gaelic Pronunciation
(excerpts)

**Donald S. Murray**

**1**
**L**

In Gaelic, the letter 'l'
sometimes requires the tongue to curl

as if it were a lever heaving vowels
and consonants with all the power

present in the lilt and lift
of the human voice. I can feel it shift

within my speech when I pronounce
a word like 'geimhleag', the sound

imitating what that term means,
a crowbar, shaft or beam,

mimicking an elbow which has drifted
up through the human body to find a place

within a speaker's lips.

**2**
**LEODHAS**

There is a gust instilled within the vowels
of the word 'Leodhas',
imitating how the wind howls
on many winter days and nights, letting loose
its power on the full stretch of the shore,
and then it stills, becoming quiet
till one can barely hear the storm any more
as it impersonates the letter 's' to which the tide
sounds similar when waves skim and stroke sand
on these rare mornings when seas turn still and calm.

**3**

**R**

Consonants made peaks difficult to climb
with terms like 'bruach, 'mor' and 'druim'
and their roll of 'r's an obstacle
as he scaled a local 'beinn' or hill,
the sheer height of the slope
too difficult for his mouth to cope
with as he sought to master the old tongue
of the land to which he wanted
so much to belong.

Alien to him as 'creagan', the shock
of these rocks
that made him falter, fall beneath
slope and summit, tongue flexing toward teeth
as he sought to pronounce sounds
of letters that brought his whole being
tumbling and falling down.

# Voices I Still Hear

**Morag Kiziewicz**

Grandpa, wore his skull cap, sang a lament,
a language I did not know, somehow familiar.
Hebrew in a Scottish accent, praised,
lit candles, celebrated Passover,
served us Mediterranean feasts.
Held loud Glaswegian debates with the radio,
never an answer to satisfy.
'Is that bacon you're cooking Morag?'

Grandma led me into the bedroom,
thought I was her school friend,
or maybe her sister Jessie.
A kind laugh, soft white hair, showed me
her hairbrush and handheld mirror with silver frame.
Still the lilt of Gaelic in her voice,
'don't end up like me',
she told me, secrets carried to her grave.

Nanny, an altogether tougher Glaswegian Munro,
fierce in her appraisal of others, encouraged
my drawing, gave me pastels, grainy paper.
Shrugged off disapproval when she
left home to work in London before the war.
'Is that you, hen?'
Never understood her daughter's anger
    left behind to care for the men.

Grandad died before I was born,
played organ for a Glasgow church,
family gathered round the grand piano.
Aged eleven, his uncle taught him to play,
his Irish migrant father died from TB.
Music, the rhythm alive in his daughter,
grand and great grandsons.
   All I knew.

# Visiting Hour

**Dorothy Baird**

In the heat of a day that demands a garden
your face is white as the sky
your skin transparent as the wax circles
you used to slide on jars
of steaming jam.

The curtains are closed, the window
jammed. Lilies *(your father's choice)*
are extravagant displays of something
I can't name. Their pollen has stained
the nurse's uniform.

You do not like their smell.

I have brought you ice-cream
which pleases you. You leave
the plate of steak and potatoes
for the cool comfort of vanilla.

*I only asked for a small portion* you say.
*That is small* says the nurse
*you should see the big one.*

Between sips of melted cream, we
rummage for words. Yours
are all frontier talk: first steps,
stitches, oozing wounds. Mine
dry up. It's not only the heat.

*You can go now* you say at last.
*Put the lilies in the hall.*
*I can't bear them in my room at night.*

# Origins of a Wallflower

**Mandy Beattie**

Whimpering
was never heard
through skin not yet
shirring-stretched but convex
hammock slung between narrow hips
After your Somme-falling there was no
umbilical ear trumpet to swallow ululations or
second sonar blip hidden in mama's womb-corner
Despite her ongoing gorge rising *they* knew
diddly-squat of my staying only of your
trimester's leaving; until *Stethoscopes*
unwaxed *their* ears & heard mama's
voice of her body's knowing. That I
was a Siberian erysimum still
clinging to the north face
& you not even a
seasick poppy

# Birthday Treat

**Bec Cameron**

Last Saturday
On our Girls' Trip to town
Auntie Fi finally lost it

We had to make a list for the Police
Of all the people she had bitch-slapped:

A Dog Owner who denied the shit had happened
A Selfie-Taker, taking up the pavement

The Jerk who jeered when an old man dropped his shopping
A Yob who lobbed a can at the leaf-blower guy

A Dickhead rolling his eyes at women drivers
 (She also kicked his Range Rover. Twice)

The Mean Cow who made the waitress cry
(Her backhanded wallop cracked the air)

The Creepy Bastard MP who groomed that kid
 (Two karate chops where it hurts)

And Auntie Fi's Husband's Skinny-ass Girlfriend
(She spat as she howled and lunged)

We missed the film, and Mum says Auntie Fi
will not be coming to the Spa, either.

# Blame the Dark

### Marianne L. Berghuis

*'It is easy to blame the dark: the mouth of a door,
The cellar's belly. They've blown my sparkler out.'*
　　　　　Extract from 'Witch Burning' by Sylvia Plath

Division, disruption, dissatisfaction - you have created *it*.
Personal power and grabbing at greed is all it *is*,
But to witness your faltering fear of uprising is *easy*.
You feast on lies while innocents die in the ghet-*to*.
Riches and wealth cannot free you from *blame*
Of the poverty, death, and necrosis that besiege you. *The*
Communities that shone brightly you turned *dark*.
Your lack of compassion eats off every struggling soul. *The*
Time is coming though. We will no longer hold back words from our *mouth*.
You must be stripped of privilege and made to pay for your mockery *of*
All women, men and families forced to choose between heat or eat. *A*
Disgrace that you are responsible for. We will show you the *door*.
For enough is enough. Our blood is on your hands, dripping and putrid. *The*
Heinous headcount of folks sleeping on streets, in shelters and *cellars*.
It can't go on that children go hungry unable to fill their *belly*.
While you're warm at home feasting from Fortnum's. *They've*
Lost hope, as parents scrapple pennies together. Wage packets *blown*.
But beneath our broken bodies lies a piece you cannot destroy. *My*
Inner core. It will not die. I grapple and grip onto this glow like a *sparkler*,
Our lights will shine bright once more. You will never snub them *out*.

58

# Reluctant Song

### Jim C. Mackintosh

It's the rump of winter in Perthshire.
Damp tones of mercurial grey poison
slothful earth, weary silver birch is
reduced to bar codes of weak light.

A blackbird, once a trusted song-ally
should have been here with me
in the slumped hush to break our fast,
the subtle change from dram to coffee

and I stare some more at the shed rafters.
If I could ask for a gift of sound I would.
Instead I return to the book holding my hand,
along the safer path of winter's seclusion.

I reach for the coat of a broken poet
who once sat with me here, some crafted
words can still be found in the soft corners
of pockets amongst sea glass and bark shard.

Her words are like a gift, each one shaped
from the shavings of life, forgiving scents
of cedar wood like an arrowed grain catch
the back of my eyes – reluctant tears flow.

How did this precious earth shrink so quickly?
I wipe condensation from the nearest pane
to see if the song-messenger has returned.
What's the point? For the poet or the living

as I sit watching and waiting for what?
A common garden bird to arrive with hope?
A squirrel, a nut-fidget to sharpen my mind
or likely the devil magpies to swell their greed.

Quiet snow returns, catching bare birch bone
in reminders of memory. Voices of derision
are buried again beneath its cold innocence.
The blackbird finds her range, snags my soul.

I am alive again.

# Reservations
for S.W.T. Southwick SSSI, Galloway

## Robin Leiper

Scattered across the map, small discarded scraps of green confetti,
little Bantustans of bog and birch, the Reserves preserve the wild,
entrusted to its proper place; here, Joni, are your tree museums.

In Southwick, our arboreal alphabet scrawls optimistic messages
along the cliff top in a sliver of old woodland. Ecological literacy
teaches us to read: temperate Atlantic rain forest, remnants of.
Oak, Hazel, an intersperse of Holly, totter on the crumbling edge,
gaze out from the old sea-cliffs, formed in a forgotten ice-age,
at the newly rising oceans; look over their shoulder, apprehensive
at the encroaching threat of Sitka. The Ash die back. Are culled.

Down on the Merse, tides gnaw at the land as tales of future past.
The rills and water-bars widen by the week. The Holy Grass, once
commonplace enough for harvesting each Spring, strewn in
churches for its sweet smell underfoot, is confined to its small bed,
pampered like an invalid. It is trusting, faithful, full of hope.

The Reeds have reservations. Rooted solid in salt flats, rhizomes
stable in the sediment, stalks dissipating the attacks of waves, they
in wisdom understand there's no stability. Everything changes.
Nothing lasts forever. They'll listen to you as you elaborate upon
your mental health. They've been informed by the authorities
this is their role in the contemporary world. They may seem
to murmur reassurances but do not be deceived. They are singing
ancient lays of mourning for the fabled, fallen heroes and hymns
to the world beyond. They occupy some unknowing borderland,
won't second-guess our futures. Inhabiting a perpetual Samhain,
they commemorate those destinies that they know are coming,
the long days of the dead.

# Alert

**Don J. Taylor**

Between motorway, rail and river
lie the disputed lands:
scratchy winter stubble,
or new-furrowed fields
unsealed against a coming spring.

Heads down, unaware,
the wild geese graze.
One outlier, only
stands elected sentinel,
head erect, swivel-necked;
the skein, tight knit in trust.

The latticed derrick looms above
thicket, ditch, and drain;
to probe the porous strata,
frack and suck earth's sullied marrow
from every rocky crack and cranny.

As night advances darkly west,
foxes nose the frozen air.
The flock takes flight
to roost by pearly creeks
that shimmer-sheen
in the oil-plant's ghastly flare.

# Edinburgh Festival

**Celia Donovan**

Dancing, an out of rhythm quick step through
the humdrum of human traffic, tour guides
touting tickets and fliers thrust in fingers,
promising papercuts and novel entertainment.
Between the tartan laissez-faire, fire jugglers
peddle flame and flare, juxtaposing
posing mime artists' paint clad patience.
Talent is scouted, plucked like a buttercup
from The Meadows. Young love gushes
from the rasping mouths of the after hours clubs.
Cobbled back streets hoard the heat, the stench
of piss and sweat cling to them with the grip
of honeysuckle. A wasp lost
in an ecstatic jig, gorges
on the slick sticky deliquesce of
a dropped ice cream cone, made sweeter
by the cry of the grief stricken toddler
swept away by the crowd, his shrill
soprano sobs deserve an
'Encore!'

# Scots Word of the Day

### Margaret Powell

That young woman on Twitter, who treats us to the *'Scots word of the day'*, takes me way back to my time living in Glasgow. It was Jimmy, my husband, who taught me the language, with sweet words that drew me in, and held me fast,

*'Ma bonnie wee lassie. Y'ir a right wee stoater.'*

At first, life with Jimmy was *'braw'*, but then the *'weans'* came along. Four wee darlings, but their *'fechting'* left me *'wabbit'*, and soon the sweet words turned sour,

'Look at the state o' you. *Y'ir hacket, an y'ir hoose is mingin'*.

Daring to answer back, I was a *'glaikit, crabbit besom'*.

He never hit me. Words were his weapon of choice.

Prepared to *'dree ma weird'*, I raised the *'weans'* and *'didnae ken ocht aboot'* his business dealings. I thought I was getting the hang of the language, but there were nuances *'beyond ma ken'*. Like the day Billy the Bampot called by, demanding to see Jimmy.

I secretly texted, 'Will I tell him where you are?'

Jimmy replied, *'Aye right.'*

It looked enough like an accident, for the insurers to pay out. I *'baggsied'* the money and did a *'moonlight flit'*.

When the *'weans'* come over for a wee visit, it's their turn to become bi-lingual,

'Dos pizzas por favor'.

It's that time again. I rummage in my beach bag, sip my sangria, tap the Twitter icon, and get ready for my daily treat. Today it's *'gaun yirsel'*.

# To the Rescue

**Alan Joseph Kennedy**

'Ewan!'

My brother's rowing boat, his only source of income besides the ceilidh band, languishes against a rusty bollard on the jetty. Its cracked and peeling yellow paint underscores the overall mood of grieving which greets me.

'Ewan! It's me.'

A frozen film of saucer-sized Lion's Mane jellyfish chokes the puckered mouth of the sea loch.

'Come out! Look!'

In the seven months since Anna's drowning, my brother hasn't left this ramshackle croft on the barren finger of land which forms the estuary's southern border.

'Ewan.'

'What?'

'A fin.'

'Leave me alone.'

'A porpoise calf. Looks trapped.'

'Like I care?'

'Let's help.'

'Us?'

'Yes.'

The rust-coloured web of iced-over, stinging tentacles confuses the animal's sonar, making it impossible to navigate out of the bunged-up outlet and re-join its family. The terrified creature surfaces to breathe. Its anguished clicking breaches my brother's bedroom, his sanctuary since that tragic Midsummer's Day swim when he lost both his wife and his unborn daughter.

Ewan groans, leaps up, storms into the tool-shed, lurches out wielding a huge monkey wrench, and strides to the boat.

'Ewan?'

'Shift.'

'What's up?'

'Move. Follow me.'

'What's the plan with that...?'
'Get on. While I row, whack it hard.'

Should I hit the dolphin or the jellyfish? My older brother just grunts. Without another sound, he untangles the heavy winch cable, shoves the boat away from the jetty, and rows like a turbine. He pants faster than the bellows of his beloved accordion, gathering dust in a corner since my sister-in-law's death.

About thirty feet out, halfway to the mouth of the inlet, Ewan whirls the craft towards the open sea and gestures for me to strike the metal deck on the stern hard with the tool.

In a flash, I understand.

'Piss right off! Damn jellified demons of Satan!'
'We're bulldozing right through, Ewan.'
'Is it following?'
'The dolphin?'
'Yes.'
'Yes.'

My brother rows without blinking until the waves grow bigger, the gelatinous film less dense, and finally collapses, gasping, over the oars. The baby porpoise soars twice into the air, the second time a full summersault, before gliding through the water towards its waiting family.

Ewan's eyes glisten, his cheeks gleam with his old ruddy hue, his lips twitch into a smile I dreaded I would never see again.

'Damn fine rhythm, baby brother. Damn fine, right enough. By the way, did you bring your fiddle? Good. I fancy thrashing out a wild jig or five once we hit land. Here, the helm is yours. Now, take us home.'

'Great to have you back, Ewan. Really great.'

# Sacked

**Nicola Furrie**

'Guid morn, may I spik tae the Ambassador, please?'

'Who shall I say is calling, Ma'am? I slam doon the phone. Fit hid possesst me tae use ma land line? I'd thocht tae find a pay phone, ane o yon anes fir tourists. Bit it wis euchert. I obtain fit I believe they ca a burner phone. Aa that binge watchin on dark nichts cums n gie handie. 'I myself am naebidy but aa hae sumthing o interest tae you an yer people.'

Fit wye I cam by it? Weel now, I spied a sandbag, oota place oan the verge. Feart o deid kittlins, I gied it a poke. Nae funny business. Yet, yon baggies lookit gie spleet so I got oot ma pockit-knife an slit the bugger open. Nithin ava, jist saun n plenty o it. A coupit it ower, an sumthin glitterin caught ma een. I pit it in a wee baggie n took it hame. Gied it a guid wash unner the tap. Scrapit the metal bitties wi an aul toothbrush. Fit the hell wis it?

Far aa the wurld, yon *objet* luikit lik a wee bellcote or birdcage. Mair intricate than ony rings far ma lugs. A hid a go on google, n wid ye believe it, there it wis n aa its glory, a match near anuff. I got oot ma faither's aul magnifying glass. He wis a philatelist ye see wi a particular interest in African stamps. Aye, sure anuff, on closer inspection there were angels engraved on the siller. *A Maqdala silver church censer from the British Museum*. Weel, that makit sense. Fit a carrie on they're haen there. Yon George Osborne – typical Tories, couldnae rin a bath.

Files, I could hae made hoose room far sumthin sae fine. Bit I kint that wid be wrang. Birdies need tae fly free an winter in sunny climes. Aye, I'd seen plinty glass cages in ma time, n no jist n *The Detectorists*. Ane o oor ain treasures, a muckle Steen, wis held doon Sooth faur far tae lang...

Rather the rare birdie bein taen by mair poachers, better it travels safe. 'Yer Ethiopian diplomatic pooch? Ideal.' Ye catch ma drift easy. Funny that, hoo folks fae far flung pairts understaun me nae bother, fan the Inglish cannae mak oot a wird I spik!

'Compensation? Nah, there's nae need far that.' 'I've been a twitcher aa ma life. Am jist glad to see oor featherit freens gaen hame tae their ane kind. Nae coopit up alangside ither sacrid spirits aa doon n the dumps.' 'Weel, that's settled then. You'll send a mannie up an I'll meet him aff the train. Gie him a dram. By the way, there's anither sack too – och aa jist left it in the field n the dubs.' Hidin in plain sight. Far ivver did I git that idea fae, I wunner? Jist let me ken fan the eagle has landed.

# Relaxing by the Pool

**Colette Coen**

'You have crossed the line, my boy. That is it!'

Hidden behind my sunglasses and my book, I listen. I'm not sure what he has done other than ask her to finish her call and come into the pool with him.

*'He's driving me crazy.* You are driving me crazy.'

He eases his body onto the edge of the lounger, trying to make himself more invisible than he already is, but he hasn't worked out the balancing point.

'Wee shit. *Look I'm going to have to go. He's tipped my drink all over the place.* Don't just stand there looking at it, you idiot. No, don't use my new towel, use yours. *I know, I don't know what I was thinking coming here for a rest. I should have left him with my mum.* A Bacardi and Coke please, senor. This wee shit spilt my last one.'

I pretend to look into the distance, but I watch as the boy pours the dregs of the plastic cup into the drain next to the bin immediately attracting ants to the stickiness. She doesn't help as he takes a couple of attempts to right the lounger. He slides into the middle section and stretches out his shivering body, trying to get some warmth from the dipping sun.

I want to reach over, tell him that he has done nothing wrong. I want to take him in my arms and comfort him. Tell him that his mum is being a bitch. Tell him that it's not unreasonable to ask her to gift him some of her time.

Instead, I turn the page of my book. To do anything more would be crossing the line.

# Refuge

### R. J. Dwyer

The girl is maybe thirteen. Her headscarf is pulled forward, but you can see a thread of acne at her hairline. She faces Rasha and talks to her. Every so often she looks at me then looks away.

She has a pain, in her abdomen, Rasha says.

Rasha's one of the good ones. When she's needed, she's there. Otherwise, she sinks back into the wall. And you feel like it's just the two of you. Some of the others are a mixed bag. They fill up our little room with their personalities. And they summarise minutes of talking into seconds. Rasha was a teacher, and it shows sometimes.

How long? I ask and she asks her.

The girl is still speaking to Rasha but she's staring at me openly now. Maybe she is younger than I think. Rasha turns to me.

Four weeks, as long as she's been in the camp. She has been twice before, and they gave her medicines, but it hasn't helped.

Get her to show me.

I stand and smile and gesture to the wall. It takes time. You have to develop shortcuts. Ways of showing what you mean. Rasha stands by her as they inspect the shelf. The pharmacy is just dregs. And we can't give away boxes, just a few pills wrapped in tissue. Sometimes we might take some cream into a syringe and give that instead of a tube. No-one complains.

She points out a couple of boxes that would make sense.

Thank you, I say, and we return to our positions.

I ask the usual questions, her periods, what she eats, her bowels, her urine. Her answers are detailed and precise.

Then I rub my hands warm. Rasha helps to unbutton her jeans and pull them over her thin hips. The bones of her ribs and pelvis stick out like tree roots. I put my hands on her belly. Ballot the kidneys, examine the spleen. Everything is normal but she winces and tenses. When she does this, she doesn't make a noise. But she turns her head away. Rasha touches her shoulder and looks at me, to ask when it will be enough.

Ok no more, I just want to listen in now, I say, showing her the stethoscope.

She seems to understand. I listen to the bowels, moving the scope. Every so often I press down, slow and firm. She doesn't react.

We're done now, I say. I look at Rasha. It's a soul pain, I say. She knows not to translate.

When she is dressed, we sit. All together again. I ask her what has happened to her. How she got here. And she tells me, more or less. A version. While she speaks, she unwraps the headscarf. She places it down beside her in neat folds and starts to run her fingertips through her hair. I should ask her how she does it, but it wouldn't be of any use. Mine frizzed out as soon as they opened the plane doors.

She starts at the top, brushing it out. First one side, then the other. Then she starts to plait. Her fingers are quick and long and thin. She sits upright with her elbows out, like a musician. And when she's done, she stops talking. She wraps her hair, unfolds the scarf, and dresses herself. Making sure to pull it down forward over the acne.

# Coronation Blues

### David McVey

Like, it's May 2023 and I'm in Europe, Paris, and I'm reading about England and the dead Queen and the new guy becoming King and I figure it would be cool to go there and join the party. I'd never get accommodation in London where the Coronation hoopla was happening, but the TV news said the whole country was throwing parties and hanging up bunting and dressing up in Union Flag suits and stuff. Then I remember Nico, my old high school buddy. He's on an exchange at Glasgow University, in the north of England, a place called Scotland.

When I climbed into the taxi at Glasgow Airport I'm shivering like I have the plague or something. Even in May, this Glasgow felt like some Arctic Russian naval base. By the time I got to Nico's flat I had to borrow a sweatshirt. I hoped he'd washed it lately. Washing wasn't always, like, his first priority.

It was only midday, but I was so tired I went to bed still wearing the sweatshirt and most of the other clothes I had. Nico shared an apartment with a bunch of other people; two girls, three guys and one I wasn't sure about. Apparently they kept bundling in and out of the room I was sleeping in, but I didn't notice them.

I woke up, still shivering, about six. Nico and me went out for dinner. In this 'West End' where he was based there were all these eateries; Nico asked if I wanted Thai or Chinese or Malaysian or Nepali. I asked if there were any English restaurants and he just laughed.

We ended up in a real student place called Gibson Street, eating Italian. I had penne carbonara and it was good and warming, which is what I figured I needed. I asked Nico what he was doing for the Coronation, and he was, like, *what?* I said, you know, the King guy, he's getting crowned and stuff tomorrow. Oh, *that*, he says.

*That?*

It turns out that on Saturday morning when much of the stuff is gonna happen, he's playing soccer - soccer! - for the Physics Department team. 'Do you want to come and watch?' he asked me.

I had kinda noticed a lack of bunting and Union Flags and street party preparations as we'd walked through the streets of this Glasgow. I asked Nico about this.

'This isn't *England*, you know,' he said.

'Isn't it?'

We settled up for the meal and walked out into a bright, breezy street with no sign of the approaching night, and even less of the approaching Coronation.

'If you're keen to see some royal stuff tomorrow,' Nico said, 'there's a place called Bridgeton. You can get a train there from Hyndland. There will definitely be Union Flags flying there.'

Bridgeton. Yeah, I might just go there. If Glasgow, England didn't want to celebrate its new King, I sure as hell did.

# All the Boats

**Don J. Taylor**

Joe and I sit on the terrace, enjoying the cool evening. I pour us each a glass of imported Ribbesdale Riesling; pricey, but as the label says, *Fresh as a Yorkshire Rose*.

Along the ridge opposite, the housing blocks emerge. Printer-nozzles swing back and fore like demented dinosaurs; lumbering freight-drones zigzag among the spindly cranes. Already, the apartments tower over the woods, on what had been my sixty hectares of rush-raddled pasture.

"They'll be seventy stories high," I say.

"Like Cumbernauld in the Sixties, Malky," Joe gives a brittle laugh. "Man, it'll be the San Gimignano of the *Lanarkshire Upland Resettlement Area.*"

He'd always been sniffy about the New Town. When I bought the small-holding forty years past, he looked over at the emerging townscape and declared it 'a vomit of concrete spewed across a bog.'

"The new flats are needed," I say. "There's near forty thousand folk up in the holding camp on the moor yonder. Land's at a premium so Holyrood has to pay me good money for the leasehold. Here, let me top you up."

Joe's joke about San Gimignano reminds me he and Marcella got hitched in Tuscany. Her Italian heritage: Rossi. Too hot for comfort in *La Bella Italia* these days.

I wasn't welcome at the wedding. An activist living on Universal Credit up in the Lanarkshire Badlands didn't fit with the Largs crowd. Ever since our university days, I felt Joe wasn't entirely comfortable with me being around Marcella anyway. She drowned last year— the November surge of thirty-eight. Herself largely to blame, Joe tells me, swirling his wine. "Ignored the evacuation order. Everything gone: the ice-cream parlour, the Dongfeng e-car franchise, farmhouse conversion. *Everything!*"

Joe managed to get out. I don't ask how.

He sweeps his arm west to east. "And all this is yours?"

"Yup. My land borders the old quarry there, right up to the line of the Roman Wall. Back then the other side was all river and marsh—a natural barrier. The Roman geographers thought Caledonia more or less divided in two by the valley; their wall like a girdle round Scotland's pinched-in waist." Joe drew me a look like I was getting all la-di-da; maybe it was the Riesling. "They were onto something, though. Now, on a spring tide, we're an island. North Sea comes in *this* way, and the Clyde creeps up from *that* direction." I point to the sunset over the Bishopbriggs Banks, just visible above the incoming flood.

"Malky, the eco-warrior, making a killing from 'Flood-outs'!" Joe shakes his head in mock disbelief.

He always liked to get a dig in.

*Let him.*

So, I agree to take him in rent-free, in return for a bit of cleaning, the odd wee job, and he's to pay his own Community Recovery Charge.

Joe's got a point, I suppose—about my good luck. Funny how things turned out. I think it was JFK once said: 'the rising tide lifts all the boats.' Well, not quite.

# All Day Breakfast in a Tin

### Alan McDairmid

I'd quite like to join the police.

My Auntie Kath says I've got the legs for it and Mum says that Auntie Kath is an expert on policemen's legs.

But here I am with, 'where's the cabbage son?'

'Fruit and veg, aisle 2. Between courgettes and turnips.' Great.

At school they said I could try SVQs. Career guidance in between Shakespeare and volleyball but really, they weren't interested if your dad wasn't a doctor or something... so, I just stayed on here.

Sometimes there's a bit of excitement like when there's a fight or some junky comes in. Grey skin and a, 'How's it goin big man?' Trying to look normal with a huge parka in the middle of summer. And you know they haven't felt normal for years. We have to keep an eye on them. Manager says we have to make it obvious as well. When they run for it, we have to go too. Manager says it's company policy. More like it's his policy.

One guy last week, all he had taken was, 'All day breakfast in a tin.' And you just know he was going to eat it cold, didn't make it out of the car park. Security floored him. Manager said to put it in the reduced section because it had a dent in it.

I had to give a statement but in the end the cops don't really care do they.

# Power Cut

**Gail Winters**

Shug knew it was too good to be true, he should have listened to Tina but why break a habit of a lifetime. All he had to do was fix the electricity meter, it was a doddle. Shug had made a small fortune resetting them throughout their housing scheme and was in high demand these days. Now that he was hitting the big time, it wasn't a surprise when he got a call to visit a large mansion just outside of Loch Lomond. As instructed, Shug was met at the back entrance by the butler, who handed him a thick brown envelope before leading him down to the cellar. Meter fixed, he moved onto an old generator in the corner, thinking back he should have said all done, that's me away but, being the professional he was, on hearing an irregular purr Shug followed the sound to a large freezer under the stairs, deciding that while he was there, he should fix that too, after all he'd been paid well. He should have left well alone, anyway that's what the Butler told him just before he struck him with the hammer. As Shug was losing consciousness, he could hear another familiar buzzing sound which soon left him in bits. Stored neatly beside the Lady of the manor, the freezer continued to do its job, this time the Butler really did do it… again.

# Nana and the Jakeys

### Jim Aitken

Drifts of pink and white blossom fell like out of season snowflakes, swirling in the warm wind of early May. They were elegantly dancing in a thousand and more dying falls. How things seem to come and go, how things you yearn for arrive and then leave, how all things must pass, I was thinking to myself as the telephone rang.

It was my dad calling and I found this unusual as he never tended to call me at this time of day.

'Is your nana with you?' he asked with some concern in his voice.

'No,' I replied worryingly, 'she was here about two or three hours ago. She came for her lunch and left saying she was going home.'

'Well, she's not there now. I've just been round to check on her. She's gone awol again.'

'I'll be round as soon as I can,' I said, 'and we'll try and find her.'

This had been happening too many times recently. My nana had been diagnosed with dementia, but she was still relatively fit and able. She had most of her family living fairly close in Leith and between us all she was well looked after. What was particularly unusual about the onset of her condition was the fact that she had become far less judgemental and critical in her manner than was the case prior to her diagnosis. The woman who would normally castigate everyone around her had become an amiable, congenial individual to be around for the first time in her adult life. While we welcomed, in a sense, the ending to all complaints, outbursts and grievances on all things – particularly related to us – we were nonetheless acutely aware that there was much more than just this mental faculty that was floating off like the blossom earlier.

We found her sitting at the Kirkgate with a group of characters she once disparagingly denounced in her pre-illness days as 'a bunch of useless jakeys.' They were now her friends apparently as she introduced us to Wee Eck and Dode. We exchanged pleasantries with her new friends and managed gradually to extricate her from them and return her back to her house.

My dad stayed with her to try and talk through certain new protocols for her, but I left and could not stop myself from thinking how it is that sane, intelligent minds can be so dismissive of others that they choose to demean them rather than attempt to understand them. My nana's brain, in part, had withered just like the brains of her new associates had by being addled through alcohol. They had something in common in that respect and I marvelled at how their lack of mental capacity had broken down barriers between them in a world that is full of fear and loathing, division, and derision.

# You Said Aye

**Margot McCuaig**

The sun is high in the sky and the tide is low in the bay below. Long strands of himanthalia elongate seaweed are sweeping back and forth in the shallow water, gently tickling the shoreline. It is mesmerising. Like you.

'Kevin asked me te marry him.'

We are at the top of the path, looking down towards the coast. The mist has lifted now, and Arran is showing off in the distance. You have taken off your raincoat and the aphid like pattern is stinging the grass.

'Jesus. Whit's that aw about?'

We are nineteen years old. You have plans. You are going to travel the world. I might come too if I'm brave enough. A week ago we lay in this very patch of grass and traced the map in the back of your journal with our fingers, lingering on all the places you want to see. I'm waiting for you to tell me that you told Kevin to piss off.

'I love him. That's whit it's all about. You wouldnae get it. You've no even had a boyfriend.'

You didn't need to say that, but it's your way of making your point. We both know I'm not interested in boyfriends. It's the impact that's your focus. I can only assume you don't mean any harm. I nod so you know I understand and agree. You're right, I've never had a boyfriend, but I don't think I need a man to give me wings. A tiny rock pipit has landed on a stone beside me. I turn to you to see if you have seen it too, but you are lost in the split ends of your hair. The bird is still there, curious in the way she is watching me, her heading turning from side to side. I meet her eye and she opens her black bill as if to speak. She changes her mind and flies, disappearing off the coastal path and down on the cliff. That could be me.

'So whit did ye tell him?' I have no reason to believe you told him anything other than no.

'Aye. Of course. I've just told ye I love him.'

You are looking out to sea, and I search for what you've found, my eyes settling on the sargassum drifting menacingly in the bay. Years ago, sailors believed that dense forests of sargassum seaweed floating on top of the ocean were monsters, and responsible for the disappearance of ships and their crews. Like the Mary Celeste. I'm not gullible but there's something in this moment that makes me feel I'm being engulfed by you. I fall into your words.

'Well, congratulations Nòra. Dae we still have time for a swim?' I'm already on my feet, tearing my clothes off. I need to feel the chill of the sea. You say, *fuck it* and join me, both of us in our underwear, swimming around the monster.

# Choosing a Book

### Susan Allen

Gladys strains to reach the blood-red spine. Her curiosity piqued by the black spiders crawling up it…not real ones, printed ones to accentuate the title, "Arachnophobia between the sheets."

Black leather fingers appear over her shoulder.

'Ahh…' she screams quietly, mindful she's in a library.

'Sorry, I didn't mean to frighten you. I wanted to help.'

Gladys gives an embarrassed titter and grabs the bookshelf to compose herself. 'No, I'm sorry…I was so engrossed in the cover I thought for a moment your gloved hand was a tarantula…and that's before I've read the book!'

'Maybe it's not the one for you?'

Gladys steps away to observe her helper. He looks about her age, or at least in the same decade, sixty something. 'Normally I'm fine with little ones – I was just taken off-guard while my imagination was running riot. After all, we are in the horror and thriller section.' Without registering what she's doing, Gladys preens the salt'n'pepper curls framing her lightly freckled face.

'I'm Tom Allan, although I may start introducing myself as Tom, Tarantula-man, in future.' Tom's twinkling eyes light his features.

Gladys feels drawn to the web of his persona. She offers her bare hand. Tom clasps it between both of his.

'Hello. I'm Gladys…'

'Pleased to meet you, Gladys. It's so difficult to pick a book from so many, don't you think?'

'Yes. Especially when I can't reach them, being vertically challenged.'

'One the other hand, I'm bottom-challenged,' whispers Tom.

'Pardon?'

Tom lets rip a spine-tingling guffaw. Gladys senses the soft hairs at the nape of her neck stand to attention. Her knees tremble. Tom continues to hold her hand.

'I couldn't resist saying that! You'd think, as a budding writer, I'd know better.'

'You obviously like playing with words,' says Gladys, lowering her lids to observe the ten digits enclosing her fist.

Tom follows her gaze. 'Oops, sorry. I'd forgotten I was shaking your hand.' He unfurls his fingers one at a time. 'Your hand is so…slight. Would you like me to take the creepy book down for you?'

'If you don't mind. I'd like to read the blurb about it.' Gladys releases a soft giggle as tension leaves her body. 'Technical term that,' she states. 'Blurb is a highly technical term used by budding readers.'

'And an essential part of a good book,' asserts Tom. His tarantula pedipalps edge the spine forward. He goes to place it into Gladys' open palm but stops part-way. 'I have an idea. Why don't we help each other choose books. You could choose me three from the lower shelves while I choose three for you from the upper shelves and we could meet at the comfy reading area to review our choices and make sure they're acceptable to each other. What do you think?'

A warm feeling oozes through Gladys. 'Yes. It could broaden our horizons.'

'Would ten minutes be long enough?'

'So long as I don't get too engrossed in the blurb.' Her excitement hackles dance.

Tarantula-man beams.

# Old Peaches

**Kirsty Crawford**

Every day I stop by an art gallery on my way home from work. I've done this every day for six years. I work in an alterations shop on the high street. I stop and stare, in the art gallery, at the same painting on the second floor. A canvas of a bowl of old soft peaches and a bluebottle.

There is something about the rusty flesh of the fruit and the glossy navy abdomen that looks so good together.

Every day I stop to look, and let my mind go blank and feel the familiar comfort of the peaches and the deep, dark green background. While all around, rows of stuffy landscape and inconsequential skill hang looking for admiration. In the height of August, I walk from the gallery to a late-night grocer, selecting the ripest peach from the green plastic baskets outside. Peregrine peaches, the juice oozing on balmy summer evenings. These are savoured moments of true happiness.

I married a man whose first wife had her wedding dress altered in the shop. She chose a satin slip with a lace cape. The thin straps were too long. She tried the dress on, stood on the grey revolving platform and exaggerated the problem. Heaving and scrunching her shoulders, leaning to each side showing us how the straps slid, exposing her small pink nipples. Her fiancé came to collect the dress, and later to drop in a bouquet of flowers from the bride. We spoke about the wedding, and he was perfectly polite, with vague answers but an inviting smile.

About a month later I took up the hem on a pair of his work trousers. A few weeks after this, the cuffs on a blazer. Once, he stopped by to ask if the dry cleaners joined to the shop would turn around the shirt he had on, with a coffee stain down the front, and a conference to make within the hour. He stood outside, bare torso underneath waterproof jacket, taking calls while he waited. Every so often, he would make pantomime shrugs through the window to me.

My two colleagues with would sniff over their work, halting animated conversations when I walked into the small kitchenette. 'She's coming,' they'd hush, through lips frozen in a smile.

His marriage ended after 9 months. He stopped me outside the shop one day at the end of winter and asked me to dinner. I hadn't stopped thinking about him since that first day. A face in the grey endless days. I was his second wife; he was my first adult relationship.

My wedding dress is beaded and clings to my hips with a soft classic veil. I take it to a shop across town and don't envy the furious needle work, to string and re-string tiny glass beads, pulling it in across the bust. Our wedding is small, his friends divided over his divorce, mine dwindling and lost back in school. In our photos, we stand in a field of fresh spring daisies, full of mischief and swelling with possibility.

During a thick summer heatwave he is hit with a virus. Long, shivering nights wrapped in sheets, betraying the warm midnight air through open windows. He sleeps fitfully, with distorted dreams and mumbles to be held. I slip in beside him, my own body protesting against the added heat. I lie quiet, sweating. Our hands slot together, and I stroke the nape of his neck until his body calms and breathing steadies.

On Bonfire Night we go to the local firework display where they let off rockets and Catherine wheels to Hans Zimmer songs. A huge fire burns a wicker man from a platform in the middle of the pond. I can see swans sheltering around the edge of the water, feathers illuminated. My husband puts a gloved hand around my shoulder and says the baby swans will be frightened and I look again and see that there are smaller geese huddling too. There are no cygnets in November. But I smile at him, and say yes, they will be frightened.

That night, the streets explode for hours with displays, thick loud booms and small squeals that disappear into the dark. We leave the curtains open and have sex over and under the crescendo of noise. A palette of gold tear drops fizz from the sky behind the tower blocks. But in the end, as I tense into the pleasure, there is silence. I hold my breath and collapse into his dark hair.

We are wrapped in each other.

There are whole months that go by, where I'm hazy with comfort and mundanity. In the evenings, I take the short way home, and check in on the peaches less often. Sometimes we meet halfway between our workplaces, in a fish and chip shop café. Over a shared fritter supper, we play three truths and a lie, and get to know the deep and the shallow parts of each other. His flair and character brings out my hibernating self, I am louder and more alive. I buy ceramic electric blue earrings shaped like stars.

I tell him about my sister, about our hiding place under the stairs and her relentless laugh when the dog used to herd us, nosing us gently, tail skiffing beneath our feet. I tell him how dark shadows on her lungs ballooned and became unspeakable. Constant hours in yellow hospital waiting rooms, machines whirring, a slow drip. We moved like clockward around the issue, but never touched the centre until there were no more hospital trips, and no more her. I tell him how we quietly moved forward, the unspoken things boiling. My father's stoicism giving way to aching silences in our house.

In the giddy gap between Christmas and Hogmanay I work hard. Great, green ballgowns falling down at the hem, satin fuchsia shirts with popped buttons, a red sequinned figure-hugger with a broken zipper.

On my last working afternoon before New Year's dinner, my fingers are flying through a final button repair on a kilt jacket. I'm disrupted by a flash of yellow and my eyes flick up. Two police officers are waiting to cross from a patrol car parked opposite. The jacket has tiny horn buttons, needing the finest black thread and in the half-second lapse, I pull the needle too hard and prick my finger. I'm sucking metallic droplets when then door opens. The yellow flashes now standing inside the room.

*Can I help you?* I ask, finger in mouth.

They take off their stiff peaked hats. Shiny black patent and black and white checks.

And I just stare at them, blood seeping into my mouth.

An accident. The weakest possible description.

He had an accident, like a child with a graze or a wet nappy. *Oops*. An accident on the road.

I sit gasping on the floor, surrounded by scraps of fabric and bury my head between my knees. In the pulsing darkness, an image of the peaches and the bluebottle expands in my mind. A place holder. This moment will pass, and my feet will keep walking. But self-protection simply fills the expanse in my head, like a magic cloth in water.

I weep and am wrangled from the floor. The light is harsh, and I can hear myself chattering. Formalities come and go and in the in-between days, time is freed from its happy structure. It drags on with endless inverted waking nights and dreams by daylight.

In the first week of a new year we have a funeral. Our short year of marriage, never embedded in extended familial warmth means I sit alone in the front row, glassy eyed. Editing the worst moments in real-time and humming just under my breath. An old habit of clawing at the shred of skin around my nailbed has returned, and I scab and pick and bleed my way through the service.

At the shop, I return earlier that necessary. I don't answer questions. I am resolved mute and absorbed in pushing my own skill. Nothing is impossible; applique ostrich feather, Gore-Tex, Bobbin lace, neoprene. I am personally requested for creations, a filming crew nearby commission a costume piece. There is an article in a glossy magazine, and a podcast request.

On the coldest nights, the high street pavement shines and the gallery is one of the final buildings to close, front façade lit up with fairy lights. The pit of my stomach, the hollow crest where loneliness festers, is softened by echoes and floor polish, and the sagging beautiful peaches.

In February, I visit on a lunchbreak. My feet fit into worn grooves on the concrete stairs, polished at the tips by years of trudging feet. Great masterpieces hang from thick wire above the stairs. For years, thousands of pairs of eyes have never looked down, looking instead with craned neck at the treasures above, and trusting that one foot with follow the next, the pattern of space and height committed to memory as they climb.

There is a small white rectangular note, where the peaches used to be.

*This painting is on loan.*

*Ca' d'Oro* means golden house. It's the first thing I see, stopping off the Vaporetto and feeling the sun bake the terracotta streets, bricks oven-fresh and pulsing. My return ticket is open, and this lack of certainty makes time feel frenetic. I walk and walk, the skyline punctuated by duomo and spires. I eat alone at a café down a narrow strada. Piles of puttanesca and fizzing cloudy lemon.

In the corner of the main square each day I notice a woman selling elaborate masks under the full blaze of the sun. In her nineties, she is crepe paper and titanium all at once. The masks are authentic creations, some with lace and velvet. Occasionally, someone brings a fraying mask, sometimes a jacket or handbag and she makes steady repairs with a care for the objects as delicate as if for a child. On the third day, I catch her looking directly at me from across the square, straight into my eyes with the black beads of her own. We stare and she smiles firm and direct, with a single nod.

The gallery is a hexagonal tower of red stone with cool air and vast dead space between marble sculpture and thick tapestry. I search calmly, then with growing urgency and find it in an alcove next to dozens of the artists other works. There is an immediate tethering, and the tight bands around my forehead fall away. An exhibition. Funny to think of the peaches as having fellows. I read about the artist and his intense political alliance to the wrong side; prison, liberty, freedom. Locked in the stables of Versailles, he started the peaches. Mind curdled with thoughts of despair he abandoned the creation in a thick mask of black paint many times, before starting again. The bluebottle a final touch, life from between old fruit.

I buy a postcard of the image and send it back home to myself. Peaches waiting for me. On another, I leave my contact details and a sketch of a beaded gown and a threaded needle. The light fading, I walk a new circuit of canals and hand the sketch card into a wedding boutique. I enquire gently at the closed boxes in my mind. One with the folded veil of my own wedding day, one with fluorescent police jackets, another with endless seeds of hope.

After dinner, I stand looking out over the water as soft air pulls waves in my hair and the great bears in the sky blink overhead. I am unravelling.

At night, I sleep in my small bedroom overlooking the warren of streets, and I dream.

Of

fireworks and fritters wrapped in greasy paper

Of

cygnets and daisies and tumbling conversations

Of

*the peaches, and the bluebottle and the thick gold frame.*

# Alki

### C. E. Ayr

'So how's your Time Machine coming along?' asks Mrs MacCallum.

I gape at her in astonishment and horror.

'Wha... who...', I demand, somewhat feebly.

I turn towards Jessica, who might be my girlfriend, but who's definitely Mrs Mac's daughter.

'It's supposed to be a secret,' I say, 'You swore on your granny's grave never to tell a living soul.'

'I didn't mean my mum,' she shrugs, 'I tell my mum everything.' 'But...', I stop, realising the utter futility of the conversation.

Telling Mrs Mac something is considerably more effective at bringing it to public attention than printing it in banner headlines on the Ayrshire News, where Jessica and I both work.

'It's no' a secret,' says Mrs Mac, 'It's the talk o' the steamie!' 'What?'

I know I'm beginning to sound monosyllabically moronic, but I feel that things might be getting out of control here.

'It's jist an expression, son,' says Mrs Mac, 'But it *is* the topic du jour at the Karate Club.' I make a noise like a nun with concussion, failing quite abysmally to make sense of the words Karate Club coming from this impossible source.

She's about five foot two inches in height and, to be honest, in most other directions too.

Her fighting weight, to use an entirely apt description, is probably around 15 stone.

She reads my expression.

'We jist call it the Karate Club tae keep the menfolk on their toes. We really jist have tea and scones and a wee blether.'

This might be a good time for me to explain some stuff.

I'm not building a Time Machine.

I'm building, actually have built, a machine that travels through time and space.

Yes, a bit like the Tardis.

Functionally, at least, that's my goal, although it currently has some, let's say, shortcomings.

Mainly that I've no idea where I'm going or, when I get there, where I am.

I just know it's not here and, perhaps, not now.

I've got lots of really clever instrumentation, with state-of-art screens showing images and locations, with date and time.

I just can't quite decipher what they're telling me.

The bits I do understand, I don't know whether to believe or not.

So I've no idea where, or when, I've been.

But, ignoring these details, I've made a couple of successful trips, secretly, of course. This is because Scotland has surprisingly strict laws controlling and, in fact, prohibiting private travel out of our own time and space.

I say 'surprisingly' because no one else, to my knowledge, has built anything approaching a working machine.

Why some idiot politician decided to propose these laws rather than something more useful like bigger and better tax cuts for the obscenely wealthy is beyond me.

But I digress.

My trips have been disappointingly dull.

I've seen a couple of fairly featureless landscapes in nondescript colours that could be almost anywhere.

But I can tell from the skies that they're not Earth.

Much more disappointing is that I've yet to see an ALKI.

My somewhat dubious acronym for ALien, Kind of Interesting.

I've seen no sign of any life whatsoever, not a bird, not an insect, not a sodding blade of grass.

But I got back safely, which is pretty important.

That's the feature I've focused much of my attention on.

I don't want to be stranded out there, somewhere, sometime.

Although, in all honesty, it's unlikely to be much worse than Kilmarnock, where I live.

You may recall I compared my machine to the Tardis.

This doesn't apply to its appearance.

Mine doesn't look like a blue 1960's police box.

It looks more like a rowing boat, the sort of thing our grandparents used to hire by the hour in places like Port Bannatyne.

This is largely because it is a rowing boat, which lives in my mum's garage.

I don't know why there's a rowing boat in her garage.

I've asked her, of course, but she's strangely evasive about its origins.

She tends to shrug, and smile quietly, and look slightly embarrassed, and shake her head, and shoo me away.

As this garage is my workshop, and it's primarily occupied by a rowing boat, things sort of evolved, I suppose.

I had to put all my clever electronic gizmos somewhere...

When I explained to Jessica that my machine was loosely based on the Tardis, she named it, or perhaps me, Disaster. Said it was an anagram.

'Whit's this nonsense aboot a time machine?' asks Eddie Lawrence.

Edwina 'Eddie' Lawrence is my boss, the editor of the Ayrshire News.

I'm not really a journalist, as she'll be first to tell you.

Or me, frequently.

I write occasional articles about scientific stuff on the basis 'you've been to the uni and that, haven't you?', as well as covering more thrilling stuff like cake sales and school sports.

To be fair to her, which isn't easy, I'm a bit of a geek, slightly scatterbrained, and barely going through the motions at work.

Because of my great passion, The Search for Alkis.

The Disaster – I need a better name for it, that makes me sound kind of feckless – is the natural result of this fervour.

So when Eddie asks the question, I flee.

Nothing I tell her will improve my already non-existent credibility. And she'll laugh.

I am in my 'workshop', tinkering with the Time and Location mechanisms, replacing a couple of chips which I hope will help me pinpoint where I am in the universe.

I don't go near the CHS (Come Home Safe) segment; I might be crazy but I'm not daft.

When I'm satisfied with my efforts I check the time.

Mum'll have dinner ready in less than an hour, so I've time for a wee sortie, test my changes.

I sit in the rowing boat, check both SK (Survival Kit) packs (I always have a back-up) and begin the IR (Initialisation Routine).

I pause before throwing the last switch, mumble a prayer to my mum's god just in case, and take a deep breath.

'Oh goody, I'll come with you,' says Jessica, stepping into the boat.

I'm so startled that my hand, poised over the 'GO' control, the on-switch, flicks it involuntarily, and everything starts to hum.

I would, if I could, panic at this point.

The thing is, once the start-up program kicks in, any rational thought process becomes impossible.

The whole structure of time and space is being manipulated all around me, a fairly weird sensation to tell the truth, so the brain slips into total acceptance mode, as opposed to simply exploding at the enormity of what is happening to it and its container, namely me.

Let me take a few moments of this 'travel' time to tell you about Jessica.

She's a lovely girl, a few years younger than me, still in her twenties, and way out of my class in terms of physical appearance.

She is tall and slim with appropriate curves, curly dark hair and a smile that brightens the world.

I'm slightly podgy, with a part-time job at the News.

I fix computers, phones, video game equipment, toasters, and anything else you can plug in and break.

So what's Jessica doing with an obsessive, almost penniless nerd, who lacks any sort of terrestrial ambition?

Well, in truth, she's probably a couple of logic gates short of a chip.

A kilt or two short of a pipe band.

I mean, she's not a cretin, but her grasp of reality can be a tad tenuous.

When the boat comes to rest I turn my head and glower at her.

This is a wasted trip, I need to go straight home again.

I'm ready to explode.

'Wow', she says, beaming with delight, 'That was so cool!' I melt slightly.

'Jessica,' I start, but to no avail.

'Where are we? When are we? Are there wee green men here? Can we talk to them? Are they friendly? Do they know we're from Kilmarnock?'

She has already opened her SK and is examining the contents.

'Hey,' she says, 'I can breathe here!'

'Yes,' I tell her, 'The Disaster carries its own atmosphere, but you need the breathing apparatus when you cross its gunwale. Go outside its boundaries. Not that you're going anywhere except home. Immediately!'

I feel it's unnecessary to explain to her that the Disaster is smart enough not to materialise anywhere totally inhospitable where, for example, the temperature would be instantly fatal.

Because she's definitely not getting out.

She gets out.

'Jessica!' I shout with some difficulty, simultaneously fitting my SCIGBA (Self-contained InterGalactic Breathing Apparatus) and stumbling after her.

She's twirling around, arms wide, radiating joy at the scene before us.

We might be in the Garden of Eden.

I gaze around at a paradise of green-blue grass and multi-hued flowers.

There are slightly strange trees and unrecognisable birds, but they are, nonetheless, trees and birds.

I forget momentarily that I'm breaking all my rules here.

I didn't check my screens to see where and when we are.

I didn't go through my usual post-landing check routine on the equipment. I always do this in case I have to depart somewhat hurriedly, in the face of who-knows-what.

I don't have a backup SK, and nor does Jessica.

And I don't really care.

She's dancing across the meadow, discarding her SK as she goes.

I can hear her singing that ghastly song from The Sound of Music.

It sounds wonderful.

She sounds wonderful.

I'm suddenly filled with affection, maybe even love, for this crazy lady.

Then it appears.

It starts as a bright glow over our heads, before dropping softly to the ground. It seems to shudder and change colour, before forming a shape which is vaguely humanoid.

An Alki, I realise.

'An Alki!' I scream.

Jessica runs back towards us, laughing and shouting unintelligibly.

I've never seen anyone so happy in my life.

The Alki turns as she approaches, and his shape changes slightly.

I say his, but I have not the foggiest if this being is male, female, neither or both. To be honest, I'm not always sure back on Earth nowadays.

But it looks more male than female (no appropriate curves), so I'll stick with that.

Jessica launches herself joyously at him, arms ready to embrace.

He points at her and says 'Bloop'.

I notice that quite distinctly, because 'Bloop' isn't the sort of word that crops up very often in conversation down in the armpit of Ayrshire.

Anyway, that's all he says.

'Bloop'.

And Jessica disappears.

I don't mean that she scarpers, sharpish like.

I don't mean she hides behind a lamppost, not that there are any lampposts to hide behind.

No, she just isn't there anymore.

I look at the Alki and ponder my options.

I obviously don't know where Jessica has disappeared to, and I'm fairly unenthusiastic about finding out the hard way.

Even more obviously, I'm terrified at the thought of reporting back to Mrs Mac that her favourite daughter (Jessica is/was an only child) has been Blooped, potentially into oblivion.

I force my second-best smile onto my rigid features, show my empty hands, and speak to him.

My first Alien contact, my first Alien communication. 'Bloop?' I ask.

Many, many years later I switch off my view-system as my grandson rushes in.

'Grandpa, look what I've got!'

He has the same sort of radiance as my son, or maybe ever so slightly less. 'Grandma built it,' he says, 'She's really really clever, isn't she, Grandpa!' I smile at him, and at her as she appears in the doorway.

I've never found out exactly what happened that day.

I've asked, of course, but she's strangely evasive about what she remembers.

She tends to shrug, and smile quietly, and look slightly embarrassed, and shake her head, and shoo me away.

But, as our grandson just pointed out, she's smart now, much smarter than before. And, since then, she's always had a strange, rather bright glow about her.

# Delivered on a Westerly Wind

**Ann MacLaren**

Simon sat at a small table in the corner of the pub, staring down into his pint and wondering why he'd bothered to come to Orkney. It was the thought of all that money, of course, and the kudos. The big prize.

He'd driven up through Scotland to the north coast - almost ten hours it had taken him from Manchester - slept in the car and caught the first ferry from Scrabster. He'd spent the day driving around the island, looking for inspiration; it was all there: the wide expanse of sky, the rolling handkerchief fields, the geese nibbling frantically at the crops, the brochs and the tombs, the stone circles, and primitive dwellings. All just as Magnus, born (as he often boasted) in Orkney, had described it in his poetry. And that was the problem: Magnus had already described it all, used up all the best phrases, had transposed nouns and adjectives, made his verbs sing. How could he follow that?

Magnus Clouston was his tutor, 'the greatest living poet in Britain, if not in Europe' according not only to the University blurb, but also the Dean of the Faculty who had admitted Simon on to the course. Magnus wasn't officially on the staff; he was there by private arrangement, so there was a supplement to be paid.

'You won't regret it', promised the Dean as he pocketed the proffered cheque. Magnus will make a Poet of you. Simon already considered himself a poet, but as the Dean pronounced the word with a capital letter, he felt the stirrings of greatness.

Magnus's idea of tutoring, he soon discovered, was to read his own poetry, in a loud Eton accent, and let the students admire it; but he did try to give helpful advice. When Simon was suffering from writer's block, Magnus said:

'Only the rich can afford writer's block. You must apply yourself. You can't just sit staring into space waiting for the words to come'.

Unfortunately, Simon had begun to have a problem with words: he couldn't decide which ones to draw on. All the words he'd ever come across had been used before, had been rearranged, had produced metaphors and similes, had become worn out and stale. Sometimes he thought the whole of the English language had become one big cliché. Magnus laughed when Simon told him this.

'Nonsense! The Turner's coming up and you, boy, are in with a shout'. He said 'boy' in the strangest way, as if he was chewing a caramel while he pronounced it.

The Turner – sponsored by Matilda May Turner (no relation to JMW, the eponymous artist) – was the university's most prestigious prize and was awarded for innovation in poetry. It could make his name. Magnus reminded him that it carried a ten-thousand-pound prize.

'Get out there and look for inspiration'.

So he had come to look in Orkney, which had inspired Magnus – the greatest living poet etcetera.

Simon headed to the bar for a refill. Two old men stopped talking to size him up and nod a welcome.

'Hid's a cauld night', one said.

They were the first Orcadians who had spoken to him. The barman was Polish, and the lady who'd booked him into the Hostel in Stromness was English. Simon was glad he had understood the old chap. He smiled his agreement then turned to study the range of whiskies on offer, pretending he wasn't listening in to their conversation.

'Weel, ah saw him gaan up Hellihole, gitelan alang in that gluffy wey o' his..'..

The barman asked for his order and Simon lost the thread of the conversation. Not that he had really understood what was being said: helly? gytelinn? gluffy? - he hadn't a clue what the words meant. But how wonderful they sounded. He took out the notebook and pencil he always carried with him and surreptitiously scribbled down the new words, guessing at their spellings. This might just be what he was looking for;

maybe his poetry would be found, not in the intricate Stone Age dwellings of Skara Brae, or the plaintive call of the curlew over the gold-green landscape, but in the everyday conversation of the native Orcadians. He lifted his fresh pint and studied the whisky bottles again.

"... rex in Mrs Isbister', he says, 'they'll mak a guid supper'. Weel, when she pit her haun in the bag it wisna saithe, it wis jist a bag o' bruck. She wis fair uim. Gied him sich a scud...'.

The rest was lost in a crashing of bottles as the barman threw some empties into a crate. Simon managed to scribble down 'recksin', and 'bruck', but there had been other words he didn't quite catch.

The two men finished their drinks and nodded a farewell. Simon decided to stay at the bar, feeling sure there would be other conversations to mine. Within minutes, three young men came over and occupied the stools at the corner. Simon put his hand in his pocket and got ready to slide out his notebook and pencil, but their conversation was exclusively about

football – and mostly about the bleep bleep manager that was holding the bleep team back. There was nothing new there. Simon hated football, and swearing but he had to admit there was a certain musicality to their tone, a Magnus-style lilt, which made him happy just to listen to their ravings. You didn't get that in Manchester. Still, he was learning nothing new; he turned towards the couple on his other side and tried to tune in. It was difficult at first because the bar was filling up, and a group of American tourists behind him were organising a food order, but eventually he managed to understand that the couple were in the throes of furnishing their new house. The woman kept repeating the word 'peedy;' or was it 'peaty'? No, it was definitely peedy, he decided, and it was an adjective. There was a peedy table in the kitchen and a peedy dresser in the boys' room and a peedy chair in the hall. He wondered if it was a kind of wood that was used for furniture making up here. He wrote the word down and waited for more, but the couple moved to a table by the window and no-one else came to stand at the bar.

\*\*\*

When Simon got back to the hostel, with too much drink taken, he was feeling discouraged. He had only six new words in his notebook. Six was not enough. He went straight to bed and slept immediately, but it was an edgy, restless sleep and at 5am he got up and sat at a chair by the window. It was already light; between the buildings in front of him he could see the comings and goings of some people down at the harbour: yachtsmen carrying bags from cars and disappearing along the pier; fishermen offloading their catch, leaving a long line of boxes at the small jetty. Neat rows of vehicles were forming a queue for the early ferry. Simon would have to catch the last one of the day if he wanted to be back in Manchester for Magnus's tutorial and the hand-in of his Turner entry. If he had an entry.

He would have to come up with something original, inventive, ground-breaking. He couldn't do that with six words. Granted last year's winner had used only five, arranged in steps across the page and producing a diagonal line that read 'hohohohoho'. There had been a lot of controversy, of course. Wasn't there always? The judges would be looking for something very different this year.

He thought again about the conversations he had heard in the bar; if some people spoke differently here, he mused, if they used unusual words, maybe others had written stories or poems using these words. There was probably a library in town; he'd look after breakfast. As he listened to the early morning noises from the street - a dissonance of cars parking, footsteps, voices calling to one another and the wind whistling through a gap in the window - an idea began to take shape. By eight o'clock he knew what he had to do.

Simon watched from the afterdeck as the ferry left the harbour, manoeuvred its way through the narrow channel and rounded the point. He felt surprisingly emotional, but whether that was at the sight of the pretty town receding from him, or at the thought of the work ahead, he couldn't say. He stayed out in the fresh air until the boat had passed the Old Man of Hoy then went inside, found a suitable seat in the bar, and waited.

When another passenger entered from the afterdeck, accompanied by a sharp gust of wind, Simon knew he had chosen the perfect spot. He opened his backpack and took out an envelope full of small pieces of paper each containing a word and emptied it out onto the table. He arranged these, in a six-by-six pattern, word side up.

In the library Simon had indeed found what he had been looking for. The librarian had shown him a dictionary of old Orkney words, which was helpful, and then she'd directed him

to a room full of ancient books – a special collection she'd said – where these words were actually used. He had abandoned the dictionary; that wasn't really what he was after.

Instead he had sifted through the pages of the dusty volumes and carefully extracted a word here and there; words chosen because they had sung in his ears and made his heart race.

When the door behind him opened again, the draught sent Simon's fragile, delicate words swirling like snowflakes around the table. He picked out the six that had landed closest to him - shander, usmal, mattle, beglan, mael - numbered them, and put them back in the envelope; he straightened out the remaining pieces of paper and waited for the next blast of air. He repeated this procedure until all the words, numbered from one to thirty-six, were back in the envelope. The last one – shalder – was almost an echo of the first, which Simon thought was a very good omen. The pattern had revealed itself.

This, then, would be his poem: six lines of six words, not written on a page, but positioned individually according to the order that had been decided by a boisterous breeze. To keep them in place they would be set between the two squares of glass which a craftsman in Stromness had cut to size for him that afternoon, and they would be held tightly together by a metal base supplied by the same source. A magnifying glass, attached to the base by a chain, would complete the display. He would assemble the work when he reached home.

It would be sufficiently controversial to be taken note of. What do the words mean? he would be asked. Whatever you want them to mean, he would reply (since he didn't know himself and, he suspected, neither would Magnus who, although it was the land of his forebears, had never actually lived in Orkney). And they would ask about the title, which he had decided would be 'Delivered on a Westerly Wind', allowing him to give an explanation of his inspired methodology. The judges couldn't fail to be impressed.

Simon looked out of the window and saw that they were close to the Caithness shore. He sat back to relax before the long drive south feeling satisfied, contented, optimistic. He was a Poet. He wondered, as the boat turned into the harbour and he made his way towards the car deck, what he would spend the ten thousand pounds on.

# Gridlock

### Colette Coen

'I understand your frustration at the current situation, but a change to migration rules, additional paperwork, and delays in reaching an agreement with all parties concerned, has resulted in gridlock. We are doing all we can to address this issue and ask that you bear with us.'

*Well, that's all very well for them to say; but they don't have to deal with the overcrowding. There really is no respite from it. I know the house looks big, what with the spare room and all, but it is my home, and I don't want it invaded. Even when I am asleep, I can hear them creaking about the place, and if I happen to be in a less than deep sleep when I turn over, I can feel them all around me. It's even worse when I have to get up to the loo in the middle of the night – an increasingly frequent occurrence. I have to be careful in case I walk into one of them in the dark, or, God-forbid, step on someone.*

'I am aware that we have been unable to provide you with a definite date when your case will be discussed. Please be advised that we are systematically working our way through our priority list, and you will be notified when we are able to accommodate your request.'

*It's really not acceptable, is it? I'm meant to live with their backlog while they hide behind lists and protocols. I can cope during the day, I have more to fill my time and I am less likely to fret about them. I think that some of them may even sneak out for some fresh air when I open my storm door and that makes the place seem less cluttered for a while. But the respite is short-lived as they seem to come back with anyone they have met during their wanderings, as if I have consented to an open house policy. How do you uninvite people you never welcomed in the first place. I really am at a loss as to how I can stop this torrent.*

We are aware that we are presently not able to offer the prompt service you are used to. Please accept our apologies along with a mouse mat as a goodwill gesture.

*When was the last time anyone used a mouse mat? They write as though I am some loyal customer who wants them to fawn over me, when I all I want is for them to actually do something.*

'I think you will find, if you care to engage, that some of your guests have skills they can offer in return for your hospitality. While I do not have their files to hand, you may find a counsellor who could help you through some of the issues that keep you awake at night. Another may be an interior designer who could assist in making the most of your surroundings. You might even find a friend; someone to share your life with; someone who will never, ever leave you.'

*Really? Is that the best you can do? Am I meant to put on a smile and pretend that I am happy being over-run? I know that people give the 'they have skills' argument, but from where I am sitting (which is, by the way, perched on the arm of my sofa as there is no room anywhere else) they are all slackers and ne'er do wells. Counselling, advice, friendship – I really don't think any of those who are here are my kind of people. I certainly wouldn't have imposed myself on anyone the way they have imposed on me.*

'Please accept our apologies for the continuing delay in processing your complaint. We appreciate your patience.'

*I am not being patient. I am the very opposite of patient. I want them gone. I want them sent back to where they came from. I know that you will tell me that they have fled war and famine and pestilence and that I should have a heart, but quite frankly, none of this is my problem, except of course, you have made it mine.*

'Thank you for taking the time to get in touch. We appreciate all feedback. We understand that our actions have fallen below our normal standards and hope for your forbearance.'

*Actions? Actions? What actions? Have I missed something? I need some protection. There is one man who managed to get in even though I had increased my defences. I added another foot to my garden wall, and I make sure that I lock all my doors and windows at night, but none of that stopped him. He started in the corner, next to the tallboy but now he always seems to be at my shoulder. I know he is behind me even when I can't see him. Lurking, I'd call it. I feel afraid.*

'In light of your last correspondence, we have escalated your concerns to our over-sight committee. We will be in touch in due course.'

*The only reason I haven't sought refuge yet at my sister-in-law's is the woman at the door. While she makes me feel very uncomfortable, there is something in the way she watches me. I think maybe that she won't let the others get too close. She does sometimes lurch forward, as though she were about to attack me, but I am too quick, and she slinks back to her resting place, slouched against the frame. I don't know if she would restrain me if I tried to leave or if she would laugh and tell me that I have always been free to leave.*

'We are pleased to announce that we are hopeful that the border will re-open within the next four to six weeks and that the processing of applicants will commence shortly thereafter.'

*It's the constant chattering that riles me. I can't even make out what they are saying. But it goes on night and day. Mumbling, muttering, chuckling, crying. I can't bear it. Okay, so sometimes I think I can make out some words; there's an odd 'hello' or is it 'hell' or 'help'. Sometimes the little ones seem to look at me in a way that demands an answer, but their pitch is too high and I cannot tune in their questioning. The only one who talks in a way that I can understand is the woman at the door. She tells me that things will be okay, although she has no way of knowing that. She tells me to breathe, to calm down, to look for compassion and find it.*

'We are aware that our intention to re-open the border last month was not met. Please be reassured that the difficulties we encountered are being rectified and that we will communicate further when we are in a position to proceed.'

*Right. That is it. GET THEM OUT. I will not accept being touched. I just won't. No way. I know that to an outsider it may have looked as though I was comforted by the woman's hug. I know I relaxed into her bosom when she put her arms around me. And okay, maybe I cried when her English Lavender scent hit my nostrils. BUT I WILL NOT PUT UP WITH THIS INTRUSION. Puffs of talcum powder floated for hours, giving an unearthly look to her companions and I don't know, maybe I recognised her voice.*

'Dear Sir/Madam/Other,

We are now in a position to deal with your request to clear your property of the 68 spirits currently residing at 21 Hampshire Crescent, Buckhaven. We apologise for any inconvenience caused and will reimburse you for any evidenced damage which may have occurred in the last six years.'

*I think there must be some mistake. They have the correct address, but there is no way that these spooks have been hanging around here for as long as six years. Six months, maybe, twelve at a push, but six years? I would have noticed them sooner. I'm sure I would have. I also don't think there's anything like 68 here. Believe me, I've counted them, although that is not an easy job due to their uncanny ability to disappear from view just as you bring them into focus. I think that there may only be around 30, so I think that the records should be checked and verified.*

'All records and numbers have been verified. Removal will commence on the 23rd. Please find enclosed a form for compensation which should be returned to this office one hour after your premise has been cleared.'

*I don't want compensation. I know what I said in the past, but I have fixed the damage along the way, and I am sure that they will leave the place tidy. I just want to ask a small favour. The woman, the one who stands by the door, the one who smiles at me when I am feeling down and shakes her head the moment a negative thought comes into my head. You know the woman I mean. You must do. The woman who smells of Yardley talcum powder, English Lavender, the powder my mother used to wear. Please. I beg you. Let her stay.*

# The Red Suit

**June Gemmell**

The red trouser suit in the shop window winked a hello at Susanna. It cast its own vivid red light onto the street below, with a hint of excitement, a flash of drama. It sang to Susan. It pulled her in. It said, 'buy me.'

Inside the shop she squinted, without her glasses, at the label. An eye watering amount, but she had to try it on. She turned this way and that in the changing room mirrors, the assistant nodding approvingly. It fitted her like a dream. The length of the trousers suited her shorter legs and the three red buttons on each cuff set it off perfectly.

Back home she hung it on the door of her wardrobe. The strong red stood out against the dark walnut furniture, inherited from her mother, which she should have got rid of years ago. The pale green candlewick bedspread, its once raised pattern now flattened with age, looked even paler against the vibrant colour of the suit. She lovingly stroked the soft material. Where and when she would wear it, she didn't know, but she shook off regrets like left-over crumbs.

An opportunity arose. She was invited to a retirement lunch, someone she wasn't close to, someone who hadn't even come to Susanna's own retirement lunch. She would have liked to send her apologies, but the chance to wear the red suit couldn't be missed.

She had her hair done in the morning, cut into a new sharper style, and bought large earrings, very different from her tiny pearl studs. The suit, laid out on the bed, caught the sunlight shining in through her window. The fabric seemed lit up from within, the colour of holly berries at Christmas. Her father had always insisted on decorating the mantelpiece at home with real holly taken from the woodland behind their home. He used to take Susanna out with him to select the best sprigs and they would have a hot chocolate afterwards, blowing on their frozen fingers. Yes, she would stand out, like holly berries. People would certainly see her coming.

She walked into the restaurant, with high heels and sparkly jewellery and paused at the entrance so people could look. And look they did, not just her own party. Compliments came her way from all quarters of the long table as she took her seat. More than one person said how young she looked. Some people stared at her a few seconds longer than usual, then turned away when she glanced over at them. She sat up straighter than normal and made sure that when she laughed her earrings jingled and swayed.

The next time she took the suit from the wardrobe it was to visit her dear old Aunt Bridie in the care home. It had been raining heavily in the early morning and now the tissue-paper clouds had thinned and parted to allow the weak sun to filter into Susanna's bedroom. The suit was quieter, more sombre in the pale light, with a hint of rose pink. She laid it on the bed and recalled a summer day when she was around ten years old. She had collected rose petals from the garden to make home-made perfume, crushing the pink blush of petals into a jam jar with a teaspoon and some sugar provided by her aunt.

It was one of her mother's 'off' days. There were quite a few. When her father died, Susanna was only nine and her mother often withdrew into a world of her own. A world of pain, Susanna realised later, but at the time she couldn't come to terms with the silent mother, eyes always on something outside the window, something far away. Eyes quick to water, living in a silence which couldn't be cut through. So, Susanna retreated into her books. Her aunt would visit and sometimes stay for a week or two when things were at their worst. Aunt Bridie, with the warm hugs, the right words and the love Susanna couldn't get from her mother. If she shut her eyes now, she could still smell the sweet roses, and feel the summer heat.

Susanna's arrival at the care home went unnoticed by Bridie. This wasn't an unusual occurrence. Susanna sat beside her aunt, sipping tea from a china cup with green ivy trailing around the rim. As she clinked the cup back on the saucer, for the briefest moment her aunt lifted her eyes, and they seemed to rest on the jacket. Maybe it was Susanna's imagination, but Bridie looked up into her eyes and seemed to recognise something there, for she reached out for Susanna's hand and patted it. Bridie's hand was small, fingers bent with age, but warm. Susanna squeezed it back.

Susanna bought a ticket for the theatre. An actor who she much admired on television was starring in a play in town. She just bought one ticket, though. During her mother's last illness, she had shut herself away a bit and although there were people she met occasionally for a coffee, there was no one in particular she wanted to go with.

She sat in her front row seat, as excited as a teenager as others took their seats. Cultured people just like her. Clouds were painted on the ceiling high above, with cherubs floating acrobatically, holding drapes between them. As Susanna leant back, facing upwards, she imagined they were moving, gliding across the blue sky which had opened up far, far above the lofty roof of the theatre.

The lights started to go down and she transferred her attentions to the stage. In the dim light her suit deepened in shade, to the colour of homemade strawberry jam. The colour of the sweet, sticky liquid which bubbled in the jelly pan at home, with rows of freshly washed jam jars ready to be filled laid out on the worktop. Susanna was allowed to write the labels in her neatest handwriting. Until she was nine. It was never made after that.

There was total darkness. A hush in the theatre. And then the famous actor walked out. He had a classically handsome face. Broad shoulders. Curls which bounced with the emotional intensity of his words. He held Susanna spellbound. In the second act he made his way to the front of the stage for his soliloquy. His deep baritone voice was perfect for the theatre. The timbre of his voice filled the whole auditorium, and Susanna's heart, with pleasure. She held her breath as he spoke, of pain, of anguish, of his secret love. At the end when he looked down at her, and only her, she almost fainted with joy.

She left the theatre and floated through the wet streets, smiling. Had he really singled her out? She had felt a connection, an electric shock coursing through her body. She felt different these days, more energetic, excited, alive. Her arms swung confidently, her hands didn't tense up in two little balled up fists, her legs took bigger strides. Her arthritis didn't bother her the way it had.

Rings with large turquoise stones now adorned her fingers. She had her hair cut even shorter. Noting what the young people were wearing, she had swapped her high heels for flat, lace up sneakers. It was easier to walk. She wore the suit every day now to cheer her up, make her feel special.

The next day she wandered down by the river where her father used to have an allotment with a greenhouse. There was always a sharp, musty smell of tomatoes picked fresh from the vine. And they were delicious. Biting into them, sweet juice had run down her chin. Her father had smiled and wiped her face as she dug with her little spade in the flower bed he had made for her. He gave her seeds to plant, sweet peas as she recalled. Soft frilly flowers with the perfume of summer. She caught a hint of that scent often now, wherever she went. Maybe it was the season.

She liked to go out in the evening on her own now, sometimes to bars. Her younger self would be horrified, but hey, life was for living, wasn't it?

The low light in the basement bar emphasised the deep cherry tones of her suit. It signalled something delicious, forbidden. The clientele was mainly younger people, but that didn't matter to Susanna. She sat at the bar and sipped from a cocktail glass as she listened to the music. It reached her from the floor, with a deep, throbbing beat. Up through the soles of her feet, until it felt like her heartbeat. Some songs reminded her of her youth, one in particular, where the female singer sang with such emotion, high notes soaring, it brought tears to Susanna's eyes. The memory of a man came unbidden, his fingers tracing her lips, his breath at her ear, whispering secrets. She had lived deep inside his eyes. For a while.

Later she wandered out to the dark cobbled street. The air was cool and fresh. The streetlights picked out the hot red of her suit. Like a chilli. A warning. No one would harm her wearing this, for she signalled danger. She laughed out loud, felt taller, stronger, invincible.

An occasional figure in the dark street ahead melted into the shadows. Single people, particularly women, moved quickly, always vigilant, but Susanna strolled. She held her arms open and lifted her face. The sky above held the stars in place. Millions of them. Tiny dots of light. She imagined she could be seen from space and smiled at the stars. Why couldn't she have been as confident as this earlier in her life? She wouldn't have had such a dead-end job and so many missed opportunities. She might then have broken free of her mother, frozen in grief, until death took her.

Susanna whirled around and the stars whirled with her. Maybe it was too many French martinis, but things were starting to spin. She could hear voices. The streets whispered her name. She felt slightly giddy.

It was some weeks before they found her in a dark bedroom crowded with dark walnut furniture, a single bed against the wall. A pale green candlewick bedspread lay over her, arms placed neatly on either side, outside the covers. Her long grey hair fanned out on the pillow, framing her face. There was a brand-new red suit hanging outside the wardrobe, three buttons on each cuff. The label was still on.

# The Walker

**Margaret Powell**

Jen had to bash twice against the door of the settlement's quarantine hut before it would open. The stench of rotting vegetables was her reward. She eased off her bags and backpack, leant her staff against the wall, and explored the room, puzzled about who would leave food to rot. Stumbling with tiredness, she caught her hand on one of the chairs. Jen rummaged for a clean enough bit of cloth to catch the blood, making a note to pack some herbs on it later, to stop the scratch from festering. Stepping outside to greet the welcome committee from this 'new to her' community, she saw that they were already halfway up the hill. Jen loosened off her cloak, preparing to re-assure them that she didn't carry the contagion, by showing her vaccination mark. The villagers stopped at the regulation distance. Two teenaged boys, a younger lad…and no smiles.

'Hi, I'm Jen, and yes, I am immune. Here's my mark,' she shrugged her cloak down to show the pale, round, decades old vaccination scar on her upper arm,

'Thanks for your hospitality,' she nodded towards the stinking hut, 'I have brought you lots of healing herbs, for winter ailments, a new way to catch and smoke fish and …'

'The Team says you've to come down right now.'

The tallest boy had that look on his face, one that Jen recognized from her decades ago job on the Force. And he looked feral. The two dead rabbits slung across his shoulders enhanced the effect. Jen intercepted a smirk between the boys, which sent her antennae into overdrive. She turned away, and pretended to cough into the rag she was holding. Turning back, she 'accidentally' let them see the bloody cloth. It worked. They stepped back a pace.

'My apology. No, it's not the Pox. Just a wee autumn cough that's going round the settlements just now. I have some plants that will sort it. Just need time tonight to boil them up to drink, then I'll be all set to come down tomorrow and share news, and exchange resources.'

They kept their sullen silence.

'Who was your previous Walker?'

'Nobody here for ages.'

'I know, you are quite far out, but we should make more of an effort to get here with news and advice. Was it a couple of months ago?'

'No. Way before summer.'

Well, that was a lie. The cluster of fresh rowanberries, on the hut shelf, told a different story. Jen took a deep calming breath,

'What can I help you with tomorrow? I see you can catch rabbits, but what about catching larger beasts?'

More smirks.

'I have great stories for the wee ones. What's your favourite?' she snapped this at the smallest boy.

'The baby lamb and the fox,' he replied, but was quickly shushed by the glares in his direction.

Jen's blood ran cold. Cassie's signature story. Cassie, who was last seen in late August, and heading this way. Jen pretended to cough again.

'I'd better get this sorted so I have a voice tomorrow. Bye, see you in the morning.'

She hesitated, waiting for the food and water usually given to the visiting Walker. Nothing. One by one they turned and walked back down the hill. She checked the height of the late autumn sun. Dark in a couple of hours. She had time to re-pack quickly, and head back along the trail. But first, she had to try to find out what had happened to Cassie.

Back inside, she emptied her sample pouches onto the table; the poison berries, toxic plants and deadly fungi, gathered for the 'warning' lecture she gave to every community she visited. Most of the Pox survivors had been townsfolk, and some were learning the hard way what was safe to forage.

'Well, that talk's not going to happen now.'

After fixing her boots, she salved her cut finger and re-packed the bags. She mashed brambles onto one of her last bits of stale bread and packed the rest away for her journey. She would snack on beech mast as she walked. It would be a couple of days, at least, to the nearest settlement back along the trail, and she didn't want to lose time foraging.

Using ash from the long-extinguished fire, she blackened her face and hands, to help her blend into the lengthening shadows. After checking the knife in her waistband, she slipped out, crept behind the hut, then looked for a safe, discrete path down to the hamlet.

Children's cries, adults arguing, this was not a happy, clappy place. In the new normal, the Tribe would be making the best of the fading sunlight, sitting around a communal fire, mending or making clothes, nets and traps. It was the chance to check everyone was well, while keeping the children safe with songs and stories. Life was hard everywhere, but most folk were doing their best to co-operate and survive. Just not here.

Jen crept near two cooking pots hanging from the metal pole that stretched across the fire. One held a soup-like liquid. The stool beside it was stacked with a pile of small bowls and spoons. Jen tried to count them. Fifteen? In the other cauldron bubbled a meaty stew. On the stool for that pot were five larger bowls. The elite of this tribe? The Team that the boys had mentioned? She did not plan to meet any of them.

One tired looking woman was walking between the cooking fire and a hut, loud with children's voices. A small wraith like dog, its rope lead dangling, followed her every move until she kicked it away. Outside the next building was a stack of spears, poles and clubs. Among them, Jen recognized a hawthorn staff, shorter than hers, with a rainbow of dangling woven ribbons. Before she could re-act, a mocking male voice from inside that hut mimicked her words,

'Bye, see you in the morning.'
'You two, bring her down now.'
'What about her cough? '
'Put a sack over her head. Cover her ugly old face. At least the last one was still pretty.'

Despite the tears blurring her eyes, Jen made it back to the hut. Knowing she wouldn't be able to fight off two young males, she arranged the backpack on the chair, then grabbed a fusty cushion from the bench. Draping her cloak over her 'sculpture', she made it look as if she was slumped asleep on the table. With a firewood log in her hand, she hid behind the door. The clack-clack-clack of a startled blackbird let her know they were near.

'Do you think she'll taste as good as the wee blonde?'

As Jen clutched her stomach in shock, her hand grazed the handle of her only relic from before the Devastation, her Uncle Howard's WW2 commando knife.

'This way to kill swiftly. This way to kill silently,' his whisky-thick voice had instructed her, despite her Granny's protests.

The knife was between the boy's ribs before he had time to deliver his blow to her sleeping 'head'. His companion, lounging on a rock outside, joined him in death moments later. After dragging their bodies into the nearest bushes, she paused and thought,

'How long before the hunt begins? I can't outrun three young males. Delay them. How?'

The nightshade berries, destroying angels and hemlock cuttings were still on the table. Between them they could bring on stomach pains, diarrhoea, vomiting, and paralysis. Worth a try. She got all of her gear ready for a quick getaway, carefully prepared her toxic harvest, then headed back to the settlement.

The women were inside the children's hut, passing round the soup. She had a clear way to the pot. Unable to resist, Jen scooped up a bowl of the meaty gloup for herself, before tipping her mixture into the bubbling cauldron. On the path back, trying not to spill her unexpected supper, she almost tripped over the starving dog. It limped towards her. She gulped down most of the cooling food, then placed the bowl at its feet.

Daylight was fading but the full Hunters' Moon would soon rise and make her path safer. She would walk until she could no longer see her way, then hide until dawn. Her gear loaded on, she set off without a backward glance. Half a mile later Jen paused. She was being followed.

This was it.

She threw down her pack, swung round and took up a defensive stance. The exhausted dog limped towards her again. She let out her breath and calculated,

'He can't keep up with me. If I leave him behind, he'll lead them to me, no matter where I hide.'

She loaded up again, unsheathed her knife, leaned forward … and cut the trailing rope from round his neck. Putting the knife back, she braced her legs then swung him, lamb-like, over her shoulders, resting his body on top of her pack.

'You will let me know when you need a wee? And like it or not, your new name is Cassie.'

Jen, carrying her new best friend, strode off along the moon-path, every step taking them further away from danger, and nearer to sanctuary.

# Behind the Mirror

**Allan Gaw**

He shivered and leaned in. The torchlight caught the glint of the fine line of mercury in the wall thermometer. The thin, silver column was already starting to shrink, and as he watched, the room temperature dropped five degrees in a matter of seconds.

"It's happening."

"The chill?"

He nodded and saw the concern on his brother's face. This was the way it always began. Every night for the last week — or was it even longer — first the chill, then the noises and finally the lights. Flashes that hurt and left an afterglow on your retina that was all you could see, even when you closed your eyes. But there was more. He knew his brother had seen it too. In the mirror. At times, it seemed just like an outline, shimmering, something barely there. But last night, he was sure he had seen a face, eyes, and an open mouth before it vanished and there was nothing left but a thick silence in the room.

"Well, tonight we're going to get a picture, Max. How else will anyone believe us?"

His brother, Ethan, was already setting up his tripod and camera. He was two years older, but they had grown up as playmates and friends as much as siblings. Here on the farm, so far away from town, they were the only companions they each had for much of the time. And since the death of their parents, they had run the place on their own. It was hard, but they were doing their best, and at least they had each other.

Ethan was wearing his look of quiet determination. His jaw was set, and the tip of his tongue was just protruding between his lips as he twiddled with connectors. He attached the cable to the camera that would allow him to fire the flash and take the picture while they were both crouched safely out of sight. Once it was set, all they had to do was wait.

Max shivered again and rubbed his bare forearms. He was sure it had become even colder, but he said nothing. He was suddenly frightened and went over to his brother just to be closer to someone, something, more familiar. Ethan looked up from the camera and smiled.

"It's going to be alright, kid. Whatever they are, they can't hurt us. And besides, you don't think your big brother's going to let anything happen to you, do you?"

Even though Max was now taller than his older brother, and both of them had left their school books behind years ago and exchanged them for farmers' overalls, he still found his voice calming. Ethan was always the strong one, the sure one, the one who would hold out his hand to comfort him and place himself in front to protect him from whatever it might be or reach out and pull him from danger. Max trusted him with his life. He knew he would never let him down.

All at once, Max felt foolish, like a scared little boy. Here he was, a grown man being frightened of…whatever it was. It was ridiculous, so he pulled himself up straight and offered to help.

"Thanks, kid, but it's all done. Let's get into position."

Both young men moved behind the old couch that was facing the mirror. Ethan had positioned the camera squarely in front of the couch, pointing it directly at the mirror. The cable was long enough so that he could operate it while out of sight. Now they waited in silence.

Max sat shoulder to shoulder with his brother but pressed his bare arm against him searching for some heat but there was none. Ethan was as cold as him. But there was no time to shiver because it was starting.

Seemingly from the mirror, there were scraping sounds like the movement of chair legs on a wooden floor. There were muffled half-noises that were impossible to place. And this time Max thought he heard fragments of lost conversation, like words spoken into the wind. He sensed that Ethan was hearing them too, and he swallowed hard trying to lubricate the tight dryness of his throat.

He strained to listen because there was nothing yet to see, and just occasionally he thought he could begin to make out the form or the substance of the odd word. However, when he heard it, that was when he really froze. It was unmistakable. From the mirror he heard his name, "Max."

Ethan gripped his arm and looked at him. Max was unsure if the gesture was one of protection or one of shared fear. But then they heard Ethan's name too. It was clear, but it was not a voice that either of the brothers recognised. And just as soon as it had been said, it was lost again in between the growing storm of half syllables, followed by the hiss of white noise that was now filling the air around them.

Ethan was still holding tightly on to Max's arm when the figure began to dissolve from the darkness behind the mirror. Indistinct at first, the form became recognisable as human, at least in shape, before there was a flash. The brothers winced at the sudden intensity of the light, and they could see nothing for a few moments. When Ethan looked back, he was sure he saw a stranger's face peering back at him through the mirror. It was obviously a man, his mouth wide open and there was what looked like wonder in his eyes. Despite the fear that was almost choking him, Ethan realised that this might be his only chance. He pressed the button in his hands, but nothing happened. There was no flash, no sound of the camera shutter opening and closing. Nothing. It was dead.

He cursed and followed the cable through the gloom with his eyes, but he knew he would need to check the connection on the camera itself. He made to get up, but Max stayed him. It was too dangerous. Ethan whispered that it would be okay, and he wriggled free of his brother's hold, and he crawled on the floor around the couch to get to the camera.

At once he saw the problem and knew he would have to stand up to repair the loose connection. His brother was watching, and when he saw him rise, he called out. He too got up, and he reached for him with both arms, trying to hold him, to stop him. As they were both briefly in full view of the mirror, there was a quick series of flashes, each one more intense than the last. Immediately, Ethan and Max fell to their knees in pain, covering their seared eyes before they felt themselves enveloped in the oily darkness. All that was left was a long, desperate silence once again.

On the other side of the mirror, the investigator drew back from the glass and swiped through the images he had taken on his digital camera to check them. He smiled because this was the first time he had managed to capture anything approaching a likeness of the two brothers.

Now perhaps he would be believed by those at the institute. The farmhouse had been abandoned since the accident fifty years before. Anyone who had viewed the property had left claiming it was a house filled with sadness. Some claimed to have seen things they could not explain, and everyone had felt the chill.

Fifty years ago, the papers had said that it was an unprecedented tragedy for the area. Two brothers, 24 and 22, lost on the same day, almost in the same minute. The younger one had slipped and fallen into the slurry tank, the older one had tried to reach to save him and had fallen in too. Neither had stood any chance. It had been a week before their bodies were recovered.

From the battered couch, the investigator studied the mirror hanging in what five decades before had been the young men's home. He saw nothing now but his own reflection in the half-light. Gone were the fleeting, blurred images of the past. Spectral echoes of two frightened young men, still holding each other, just as they had died.

He started to dismantle his equipment — the cameras, the lights, the microphones, along with the powerful computer to which they were all connected. He was sure he had a complete record this time of the temperature and pressure fluctuations, the indistinct sounds, even the muffled voices, but it was surely those final photographs that would clinch the report.

Already the room was warming. Three, four, now five degrees according to the digital thermometer he had set up. It was to be expected. Whenever the ghosts of the brothers faded back into the darkness from wherever they came behind the mirror, the room could once again briefly become what it had always been — just part of an old, empty house, but one filled to overflowing with the past.

# Supermarket Starlings

**Norma-Ann Coleman**

In the supermarket car park an early bird employee was unlocking rows of trolleys ready for the arrival of the day's marauding shoppers.

'Cock-a-doodle-doo, cock-a-doodle-doo.'

He was puzzled as the nearest farm was miles away so what was a cockerel doing in the car park?

Another early bird cackled. Proud of his mimicking skills, Yar loved causing confusion and the human's obvious bewilderment was a bonus. Yar's main job was knocker-upper, and he enjoyed scaring his fellow starlings with a new alarm call. Today several young birds were so startled by his cockerel impersonation that they fell off their roosting branches and then, embarrassed by the flock's hoots of laughter, flew back pretending they had meant to vacate their perches all along. Seamus the scribe got such a fright he almost dropped his quill pen and even Pythia the soothsayer-starling snorted in disapproval though that was probably because she had been awakened prematurely from one of her deep trances.

'There's far too much unseemly chitter-chatter going on,' an authoritative voice intoned. 'Order, order. Morning assembly is about to commence.' The voice belonged to Wingco, a five-star starling with countless successful flying missions to his credit. All beaks returned to silence mode.

'Yar, you are incorrigible,' Wingco said.

'Thank you Wingco,' Yar replied looking as sheepish as a starling could look.

Shaking his head, Wingco proceeded with the first item on the agenda: food availability. 'With winter approaching,' he said 'insects are in short supply, but scouts have reported a substantial quantity of berries in hedgerows to the south. As usual, waste vegetables and fruit are plentiful right below us in the supermarket car park though scavenging crows and gulls may be a problem. If so, it will be a good opportunity to practise mobbing skills to scare off any rivals - but try to avoid being pecked.'

Wingco then called on Tomasz, the weather forecasting egghead to give his daily report. Tomasz perched in front of a leaf on which he had scrawled all sorts of strange hieroglyphics which nobody but himself understood. 'I expect fine flying conditions to last all day with clear skies and just enough wind to make it interesting.' Tomasz, a bird of few words, always seemed relieved to complete his report and return to his charts.

'May I just add Wingco', said a bird with striking multicoloured feathers who was known as the Doctor, 'that as a result of yesterday's heavy rain, there are puddles to the south-west of the car park that are deep and wide enough to allow several starlings to bathe at the same time. Bathing is jolly good for the pectoralis muscles, major and minor, of course and…'.

'Thank you, Doctor,' Wingco interrupted him swiftly. 'Let's not get too technical. I prefer to think of bathing as an art form for us starlings, and splashing in unison is excellent training for the aerial movements of grace and fluidity expected of us. But don't take too much out of yourselves. I want you in tiptop nick for tomorrow because,' Wingco paused for effect, 'tomorrow is the Big Day. Bathing and gentle exercise will suffice today and at dusk tonight we will have a shorter than usual session of aerial manoeuvres before roosting. Then after a good night's sleep - and no unnerving alarm calls please, Yar - we will take off in wing tip formation, meet up with the other contingents of supermarket starlings from our region and fly to the mega roosting competition site. We've trained hard and I know that this time we, the Supermarket Superstars, can beat the Galloway Galaxies in the Grand Murmuration. We lost narrowly on points to them last year as our synchronised swooping wasn't quite good enough but with the new moves we've developed surely glory will be ours.'

Wingco's words were received with wild clapping of wings and cacophonous chackerchackerchackering.

Such was the general excitement that the next morning most birds were awake before Yar. Wingco kept things low-key at

Assembly. 'All good on the weather front,' said Tomasz and the Doctor pronounced every bird fit and ready to go.

'Pythia, do you have a prophecy for us?' Wingco asked. The soothsayer came forward and spoke in the tone of the entranced.

*'Success is assured for those who paint the sky with whispering feathers
more and more till the air is alive with the music of gushing water
swoop and wheel and whirl into an undulating sea
of shape-shifting tapestries, dark but lustrous as the moon.'*

As one, the starlings tapped their beaks on the branches in respectful appreciation. A youngster asked his father how you could be dark and lustrous at the same time but was pecked for his insolence.

Inspired and determined the flock took off. One by one all the other groups of supermarket starlings joined them and by the time they reached the Grand Murmuration site the enhanced flock was an impressive sight indeed. The Galloway Galaxies had already arrived, brimming with the confidence of champions.

'I'd love to take them down a twig or two,' Wingco said to no-bird in particular.

As dusk approached the three competition judges flew on to a platform on the highest tree. 'As is our custom,' the Senior Judge proclaimed, 'the challengers will fly first. Their performance will be marked by each judge and the scores placed in the sacred nest. There will be no conferring. The same procedure will be employed for the current champions. Then I shall scrutinise the scores and declare the winner.'

The two captains, Wingco and Vidian from the Galloway Galaxies shook wings. And the chitter-chattering of the large crowd died down as the MC-bird perched on the podium.

'Fellow starlings,' he cried, 'I give you the challengers, the Supermarket Superstars.'

Fifty thousand avian artistes arose, forming an intricately coordinated pattern. They painted the sky with whispering feathers till the air resounded with the music of gushing water, then swooped, wheeled, and whirled into an undulating sea of shape-shifting tapestries, dark but lustrous as the moon.

The Grand Murmuration had begun.

# The Gold Bar

J. D. Allan

When I was eight, I visited a gold mine on the outskirts of Johannesburg on a school trip. At the time, it was the deepest mine in the world. My memory of descending into the earth is hazy. Details like how humid and noisy it was has stayed with me, but little else. It's what happened after we resurfaced that has stuck in my mind. We were led into a room with a small, covered table at the centre. On the table was a trapezoidal-shaped gold ingot, glowing lustrously. Standing behind the table was a man wearing white gloves. This immediately put me in mind of Mickey Mouse. I'd often wondered why Mickey, Goofy, and Donald Duck wore white gloves. Many years later, I'd learn that the early animators of the 1920s imitated the popular vaudeville traditions of the time, minstrelsy in particular. Mickey Mouse was essentially borne out of racist parody.

'Goeie middag, kinders,' said the man. He gestured at the ingot like a magician. 'Can anyone tell me why gold bars are shaped this way?' There were no takers. 'Everyone is shy today. That's okay.' The man paused for a moment, taking in his audience. 'In front of you is twelve and a half kilograms of the highest karat South African gold, worth many hundreds of thousands of rand. If any of you can pick it up, you can keep it.' Wide-eyed glances darted around the room. 'No trick. If you can lift the gold from the table, it's yours.' The man beckoned us forth with his cartoon hands. 'Come, come. Give it your best shot.' Our teacher arranged us in a line. One by one, my classmates attempted to lift the gold bar. Little hands and fingers pushed and pulled, but none could make it budge. The ingot's smooth sloping sides made it almost impossible to get any kind of purchase on it. I convinced myself I would be able to lift it if only I could upend it in some way. I had an idea. If I knocked the table over, I might be able to catch the gold bar as it fell. I was already fantasising about what I would buy with my new wealth: a crate of Chomp bars, an Asteroids arcade machine, Evel Knievel pyjamas complete with cape. My turn in the line came. As I approached, I pretended to trip. I turned, and with a fair bit of force, I swung my hip into the side of the table. It didn't yield in the slightest. Pain ripped through me like electricity. The man let out a deep belly laugh. 'Ho ho ho ha ha ha!' I was doubled over holding my side, trying desperately not to cry. The man lifted the table cover. 'Look, look,' he said gleefully. The small table had heavy steel legs bolted to the floor. 'What's your name, seuntjie?' asked the man.

'His name is David,' interjected the teacher. 'He's our wee Scotsman.'

'Ah. A canny Scotsman. That explains it.' The man ruffled my hair a little too vigorously. 'A good try, Scottish, but you have to get up with the crow to catch out an Afrikaner.' I hadn't the faintest idea what that meant. All I knew was that my hip ached, and I wanted to go home. 'Gather round, kinders,' announced the man. 'In recognition of David's effort, we're going to let him hold the gold bar.' The man squared my shoulders and positioned my hands, palms up. With his back to us to obscure his method, he lifted the ingot from the table. He turned and placed it in my hands. The gold was cool, sleek, and luminous, but most of all, heavy. Too heavy for an eight-year-old, perhaps. Because I dropped it. Right on the man's foot.

# A Story of Bones

### Mary Irvine

The sombre look of the lady sitting on the other side of the desk froze into disbelief. Em could almost imagine her hand reaching for a panic button under the desk.

'Bones.'

It was neither a statement nor a question...

'Yes!'

Em's resolve to keep it simple somehow dissolved. She tried to maintain a serious tone, as the subject matter demanded.

'Well, not actually a skeleton as such. Just…bones - a dismembered skeleton, in fact.'

This was just one more staging post on a protracted journey to lay her friend finally to rest. For most people the burial of a loved one – or an unloved one for that matter - and the knowledge that they were now 'at peace' was the first step in an indeterminate grieving period. Not for Em, though, living on a small Greek island. The sudden death of her friend and the initial burial was the beginning of a journey she had never envisaged having to undertake. Em knew the dead in Greece – and possible other cultures – were not allowed to have an immediate final resting place. The ceremony of 'the lifting of the bones' could take place anytime from one year after the initial committal. The lifting depended on two factors. First, the climate - a lot of rain helped for an 'early' lift. Second was the need for space. Severe winters could lead to an upsurge in demand.

She had heard, from others, of this custom. A custom which often generated quite horrific stories of what the removal involved –

'…looking as he did when we buried him two years ago.'

Or,

'…it was only a year, and he wasn't ready. We had to re-bury him.'

The latter comment referred to the removal of the body on a sort of wheelbarrow, for re-burial, to another spot in the hallowed ground, reserved for just such an event. The wife and oldest daughter of the deceased followed, one laughing at this grotesque whilst the other alternatively laughed and cried.

Or the aged crone, who, during the 'lifting' of her husband's remains, decided to help with the disinterment by scrabbling in the earth and then shouting,

'I've got the skull!' holding it up for all to see. This caused her daughter-in-law, a foreigner like Em, to disgrace herself with inappropriate, if nervous, laughter. She was never forgiven.

It was not uncommon for bodies 'not to be ready.' Modern drug treatment tended to preserve the flesh- especially in the case of cancer patients. However, a small amount of flesh adhering to the bones was quite acceptable. That would detach itself from the bones during the cleansing process. Em felt she didn't need to know further details of this ceremony.

Em had not planned this visit to the undertakers', although it was 'on the list'. She had gone to the library in the centre of town and happened to park in an area that involved passing an undertaker. Why not? It would have to be addressed soon. The undertaker's trim figure, encased in a black pencil skirt, decently covering her knees, as behoved her job, and a modest, white, cotton blouse with frilled frontage and a neckline only just low enough to reveal a gold chain, had led the way into a small room, well-lit by natural light. She had listened without comment as Em had begun to explain. Em always found it difficult to begin so, in the light of former experiences with the various official bodies consulted on bringing the bones back to the UK for cremation, she had tried a different approach.

'I'm not a nutter, this is not a wind-up and you're not on Candid Camera.'

In retrospect, not the best opening, Em had thought. She continued, as dispassionately as she could, to explain that she wanted to know how much it would cost to arrange the cremation of a box of human bones.

Em having explained more coherently, the lady acknowledged the novelty of the situation and telephoned the superintendent of the local crematorium. When she had finished speaking the silence from the other end resounded deafeningly round the room. Em then heard a muffled voice with the occasional non-committal 'Yes' or 'No' at her end. The handset gently returned to its cradle; the 'phone being an old-fashioned type adding to the general ambience.

'He doesn't know. He's never come across this situation before. He'll have to consult Head Office.'

Surely, not 'Him' Himself, sprang to mind but Em managed to prevent any verbalisation of such a facetious comment.

Some days later, driving along the coast road Em saw a sign indicating a crematorium. A moment's decision resulted in her walking through a number of men in evening dress, wearing colourful sashes. Some of them even sported what looked like aprons, although not of the practical kind. The superintendent quickly ushered Em into his office. Again a glazed look. Again 'I've never heard of such a situation.' He advised her to contact the Scottish Office. Em slunk out, fully expecting men in white coats would be waiting outside to get her sectioned.

She sat in the car and breathed heavily. Would this journey ever reach its destination? The initial problems in Greece had been solved in their own 'traditional' manner and, for once, Em was grateful. The relevant documents from there were even legal – eventually!

Next had been the British customs. During transit, at Heathrow, Em had had a couple of hours to kill before her flight home. She opened the door marked 'Customs' and entered a cubicle-sized room with a narrow counter either side of a Perspex divider. A raised button was labelled 'Press for Assistance'. She did as it requested. Almost immediately, a side door opened on the other side of the Perspex and a tall young custom's officer, sporting a deep blue turban and a neatly trimmed full beard, smiled welcomingly.

'Yes?'

Em explained the Greek custom and that she wished to fulfil a promise to return her friend's remains to the UK for cremation. The young man assumed the face and attitude of sympathy.

'You need to arrange transportation of the coffin with an airline and the...'

Em's face stopped him in mid-explanation…

'Yes?'

'It's not a coffin… it's a box of bones about this size', Em indicated with her hands.

'One moment, I'll go get…'.

He was gone through the door. A few minutes and a more mature officer entered. He exuded an air of polite authority.

'Now, madam. How may I help you?'

Em explained. Obviously, nothing fazed this gentleman.

'Mm. New one that. But no problem. Write to the Head Office and they'll see you get the appropriate form.'

Em rushed her thanks and withdrew.

Other difficulties had followed but she had ridden them all, often resorting to black humour as a way of coping. No-one, but no-one, had encountered this situation before. Em imagined later conversations in offices and round dinner tables. Conversations of disbelief, shakes of the head, expressions of sympathy and then the jokes.

The final visit had been to the Scottish Office in Edinburgh, a three-hour train journey. 'Phone calls had been made, emails exchanged, and copies of all necessary certificates sent, so the situation was fully understood. The appointment had all gone relatively simply. Simply compared with previous officialdom. Efficiently, and with appropriate sympathy, the letter giving permission for the cremation had been duly handed over.

On the way back to the station Em called for a coffee. She pulled out the letter to read. Her heart sank. There were two errors, obviously due to meaning being lost in translation. The name and the age of the deceased were wrong. Minor errors but ones that may cause problems. Coffee finished. Back to the Scottish Office. Em explained the mistakes, and, with quiet efficiency, another letter was duly typed and stamped. This time Em checked the letter upon receipt. She had returned home and placed the envelope with all the others.

She could do nothing more than wait.

Now, nearly eight years later, the news had come. The nuns were lifting the bones. Em prepared to collect them. She could finally close that chapter of her life – apart from the very secret memories. Then the bombshell.

Em had always been careful to refer to the bones being 'returned home', but the nuns had discovered the cremation element. They were not best pleased. Em was committing a most grievous sin. Would handing over the bones make them complicit? Em knew the words that the bones would speak, were that possible. But, she had made a promise and she always, but always, kept her promises. Em prepared to do battle once more

She made her plans, booked her ticket, arranged accommodation. All was in place. She rang the Superintendent to arrange the cremation. Within hours he rang back.

'I am so sorry. Legally it can't be done. There's nothing to cremate.'

She went to the island. She went to the cemetery. The grave was empty. The nuns showed her the bones in their box. These were not her friend. They did not laugh with her and sing for her. The island had given him life and now was claiming him in death. But she had their friendship to keep. That she would carry with her, wherever she went. She smiled as she watched the nun replace the box in its niche, turned and walked back down the hill.

# *ANTHOLOGY ORDER*

## Vernal Equinox Winners

| Page | | |
|---|---|---|
| 2 | James Bradley | A Playground in Beijing |
| 3 | David Mark Williams | Blue Garden |
| 4 | Gillian Dawson | Temporal Shift |
| 5 | Marcas Mac an Tuairneir | Gaoir na Gaoithe |
| 6 | Marcas Mac an Tuairneir | The Screaming Wind |
| 7 | Ceitidh Campbell | Brot |
| 8 | Ceitidh Campbell | Soup |
| 9 | Donnchadh MacCàba | Cùl-Sleamhnachadh |
| 10 | Donnchadh MacCàba | Back-sliding |
| 11 | Stephen Eric Smyth | Homework 2040 |
| 13 | David Bleiman | Dreich, Dour an Drouthy |
| 14 | Hamish Scott | The Alcomie o Curlin |
| 15 | Fiona Curnow | Angie Babe |
| 21 | Claire Demenez | My Birds |
| 26 | Harry MacDonald | Room 12, The Dissection of Anna J Aged 101 |
| 28 | Tracy Geddes | Tangled Up |
| 30 | Lesley Traynor | Walking with Shadows |

## FWS Selected Writers

| | | |
|---|---|---|
| 33 | Shasta Hanif Ali | Rootlessness |
| 34 | Anne Pia | Anthem |
| 36 | Morag Smith | Pylon Pals |
| 38 | Stephen Watt | Mink |
| 40 | Gordon D. W. Scott | A Caunle for Chairlie |
| 41 | Damaris West | Hand-feeding Birds in Rozelle Park, Ayr |

| | | |
|---|---|---|
| 42 | Jane Lamb | Pacitto's |
| 43 | Ceitidh Campbell | Rèis Bhun-os-chionn |
| 44 | Ceitidh Campbell | Upside-Down Race |
| 45 | Jim Aitken | Future Investments |
| 46 | Ian McDonough | Fruit |
| 47 | Victoria Maciver | Gairm |
| 48 | Victoria Maciver | A Call |
| 49 | David Betteridge | A Sure Place |
| 50 | Donald Saunders | A Cast for the Numbers |
| 51 | Karen Hodgson Pryce | The Torrent |
| 52 | Donald S Murray | Guide to Gaelic Pronunciation (excerpts) |
| 54 | Morag Kiziewicz | Voices I Still Hear |
| 55 | Dorothy Baird | Visiting Hour |
| 56 | Mandy Beattie | Origins of a Wallflower |
| 57 | Bec Cameron | Birthday Treat |
| 58 | Marianne L. Berghuis | Blame the Dark |
| 59 | Jim C. Mackintosh | Reluctant Song |
| 61 | Robin Leiper | Reservations |
| 62 | Don J. Taylor | Alert |
| 63 | Celia Donovan | Edinburgh Festival |
| 64 | Margaret Powell | Scots Word of the Day |
| 65 | Alan Joseph Kennedy | To the Rescue |
| 67 | Nicola Furrie | Sacked |
| 69 | Colette Coen | Relaxing by the Pool |
| 70 | R. J. Dwyer | Refuge |
| 72 | David McVey | Coronation Blues |
| 74 | Don J. Taylor | All the Boats |
| 76 | Alan McDairmid | All Day Breakfast in a Tin |
| 77 | Gail Winters | Power Cut |
| 78 | Jim Aitken | Nana and the Jakeys |
| 80 | Margot McCuaig | You Said Aye |
| 82 | Susan Allen | Choosing a Book |
| 84 | Kirsty Crawford | Old Peaches |
| 90 | C. E. Ayr | Alki |

| | | |
|---|---|---|
| 97 | Ann MacLaren | Delivered on a Westerly Wind |
| 103 | Colette Coen | Gridlock |
| 107 | June Gemmell | The Red Suit |
| 112 | Margaret Powell | The Walker |
| 117 | Allan Gaw | Behind the Mirror |
| 121 | Norma-Ann Coleman | Supermarket Starlings |
| 124 | J. D. Allan | The Gold Bar |
| 126 | Mary Irvine | A Story of Bones |